Persuading Lucy

Tammy Mannersly

The characters and events in this book are fictitious. Any similarity to real persons, living or dead, places, or events is coincidental and not intended by the author.

If you purchase this book without a cover you should be aware that this book may have been stolen property and reported as "unsold and destroyed" to the publisher. In such case the author has not received any payment for this "stripped book."

Inkspell Publishing
5764 Woodbine Ave.
Pinckney, MI 48169

Edited By Vicky Burkholder
Cover art By Najla Qamber

DEDICATION

To Beck
Thank you for accepting my weirdness as only a best
friend can. Your friendship has been and always will be
precious to me.

CHAPTER ONE

Juggling three glasses and a bottle of white wine, Lucy Spencer wove her way through the crowd engulfing the Riverside Tavern on Friday evening. As she tried to push quickly through the throng of obstinate people, she immediately regretted having chosen to wear her bandage dress to the occasion. She hadn't been out for drinks with her work friends in a long while and had been trying to make an effort with the green figure-hugging number.

When she finally reached their table, Lucy breathed a sigh of relief, free from the lively horde. Then, at the sight before her—heads bowed low over an electronic device—she frowned and quickly noted her mistake. Leaving her mobile phone alone on the table now seemed an obviously poor decision. She had thought it would be safe for a few minutes, but that had proved time enough for her good friends to snoop.

Lucy gently placed the glasses on the tabletop and began to pour the wine, trying desperately to ignore the uneasy feeling filling her stomach. Rosie's bleached blonde curls and plump cleavage bounced as she glanced up quickly to greet her. With a grin teasing at her rouged lips, Rosie nudged the taller, lankier young woman beside her with an elbow. Steph's colorful pixie cut was still bowed over Lucy's phone for a moment longer and then she glanced up to aim a sharp smirk across the table.

With a careful push from her index finger, Steph slid the device closer to Lucy. "Luce," she said innocently. "What's a *bome*?"

A flock of overly energetic butterflies buzzed around in Lucy's gut. She had hoped to keep at least this secret separate from her working life. Nerves got the better of her and it became difficult to swallow. Making an effort to appear nonchalant, Lucy brushed the straight chocolate strands of her shoulder-length bob free from her neck.

Steph quirked an eyebrow at the action and her expression became playful. "And why does he miss *playing ninja* on the beach volleyball courts?"

Rosie spat out a laugh and snorted, which only encouraged Steph to release the quiet chuckle she'd been trying to contain.

"Okay. Okay." Lucy perched her slender figure on an empty barstool and then raised her hands to silence them. "Ha-ha. It's all very funny, but it's not what you think."

She spun her mobile phone around and glanced at the screen. Several messages in a conversation with her best friend Maddy appeared.

Maddy: *Your loving bome has called again, begging for your phone number. Apparently, he had a dream about the old days. You two playing ninja on the beach volleyball courts or something. He said he misses it. He misses you. Anyway, call me.*

Lucy: *Tell him he can take his fond memory and shove it up his womanizing ass!*

Maddy: *Are you ever going to talk to him again? You know he still doesn't know why you stopped.*

Maddy: *Luce? Maybe I should just give him your new number and be done with it.*

Lucy swore and her two friends were lost to hysterics once more.

As she madly messaged Maddy back, Lucy noticed

Steph move forward, the fabric of her black Ponte jacket creasing as she leaned her elbows on the table. Even though she tried not to be obvious, Lucy was sure Steph had seen the reply *"don't you dare"* before it had been sent out into the universe.

"So, are you gonna confess or what, Luce? Who is this guy she's talking about? And what is a *bome*?"

Lucy sighed in frustration and placed her mobile phone back on the table. She frowned up at Steph and then rolled her turquoise-blue eyes. "Bane of my existence," she said.

Steph's curious expression brightened, and she relaxed her long, wiry frame back into her seat.

"Clever," cheered Rosie.

"So, out with it? Who is he and what's the deal?" Steph rubbed her hands together eagerly.

A heavy dread seemed to weigh against Lucy's insides as she realized she didn't have much choice in the matter at hand. She could tell the girls now or put up with their constant inquiries every day at work until she caved. Knowing them well meant Lucy knew they wouldn't give up until they had enough gossip to satisfy them. Releasing an almost never-ending sigh, Lucy resigned herself to the task.

"He—the bane of my existence—is an old former friend of mine. We became friends in middle school. We were best friends until senior year and then I cut off all contact with him when I went to college."

Shifting her short buxom figure to the edge of her chair, Rosie leaned her elbows on the table and frowned forlornly. "What happened?"

"It must have been something pretty crappy for you to shun him in such a way," Steph said before taking a sip from her glass of wine.

Lucy looked down at where her hands rested on the table. Unconsciously, she had begun to pick at her fingernails—not ripping, but fiddling. Just thinking about the reason aroused feelings of anger and betrayal. The emotions washed over her, burning through her as if the situation had happened only yesterday, not nearly a decade and a half ago. She took a deep breath and blurted out the transgression.

"I'd thought we were friends. Great friends. Then he started to make his way through my girlfriends, dating one by one as if it were a sexy schoolgirl smorgasbord. He would never date any one in particular for a long period of time, but almost always left a broken heart in his wake and a crying mess that I had to clean up."

"What a bastard," spat Rosie.

Steph narrowed her gaze. "And never once did that include you?"

Lucy frowned. "We were just friends."

Glancing from Steph to Lucy, Rosie shrugged. "Friends date."

Rolling her eyes, Lucy looked away and over the crowd around them before taking a sip of her white wine in an effort to quell her annoyance at them forcing her to both remember the painful situation and then explain it. After many months of refusing and being too preoccupied with work, she had finally agreed to go out for drinks with them, taking the tram from their offices in Elizabeth Street to Melbourne's lively Southbank precinct. Yet, never had it crossed her mind that their enjoyable outing might have become an inquisition.

When she glanced again at Rosie and Steph, they were still staring at her intently, obviously waiting for further explanation.

"What?" Lucy growled, irritated at how quickly the conversation had switched from the girls being indignant on her behalf to her past affair intriguing them.

"Out with it," demanded Steph as she tapped her index finger on the table to illustrate her impatience.

"No. We never dated."

Rosie eyed Lucy carefully. "But you would've liked to?"

Lucy glared at them angrily. "I would've liked for him

to have kept it in his pants where my friends were concerned or at least to have had the decency to date one seriously and respect our friendship. But clearly that was too much to ask."

"Sour grapes, much?" Rosie teased her.

Finding courage in alcohol, Lucy gulped the rest of her wine before giving them both a fierce death stare, but Steph and Rosie were unfazed. They seemed to be enjoying themselves greatly at her expense.

"In case you've lost the plot a bit, you're both women and my friends, therefore you should be on my side not his."

"Oh, we are, Luce," Steph said with a grin. "It's just that this is the first time in the five long years I've known you that I've seen you get hot under the collar about some guy."

"So true," Rosie agreed. "I'm not even sure you've had a date in the three years I've worked with you."

"Thanks, guys." Lucy scoffed at them. "You make me sound like a cold, sexless spinster. And what about Trent or have you both just conveniently forgotten about him?"

"Trent doesn't count," said Steph.

"Yeah," Rosie agreed. "You met up for coffee like twice and made dinner reservations that you never kept."

"You were too busy with work," Steph interjected. "You're *always* too busy with work."

With a wave of her hand, Lucy dismissed them and their unhelpful criticisms. She loved being an executive at Insight Marketing and had worked very hard to get to that position. Just because her colleagues didn't appreciate her passion and couldn't understand why she thought working was more important than dating, didn't mean she was about to waste any energy trying to convince them otherwise.

"Whatever, ladies. Thanks for the lack of solidarity."

"Don't be like that, Lucy-cakes." Steph reached out and covered Lucy's hand with her own. "We really do love you, babe, and of course, we hate that douchebag who screwed all your friends and hurt you."

"Really, we do," Rosie concurred, her cheeky smile becoming sincere. "It's just, we don't often see you so passionate about something other than work. Guess it just took us by surprise."

Lucy considered their expressions carefully, seeing the earnestness in their eyes and then shrugged. "I understand. Unfortunately, the mere subject of him sets me on edge. I can't believe he still infuriates me so much after all these years."

Steph quirked an eyebrow at Lucy, but then nodded thoughtfully.

Rosie took a sip from her glass of wine, swallowed and then let out a sigh. "So, he really was a right bastard then?"

Lucy nodded. "A real piece of work. He still doesn't understand what he did or why we stopped talking. I guess being God's gift to women and all means he just doesn't have to feel responsible for that kind of thing."

"What a jerk," said Steph as she finished the last of her wine. Standing up, she wiggled her empty glass in front of the others. "Who's ready for another?"

***

Although he tried, Callum Hawthorne just couldn't seem to give his woman-of-the-week, Natalie—or was it Naomi?—his full attention. One moment, he was glancing outside at the people wandering along the Southbank Promenade beside the Yarra River and the next, he was looking back inside, watching the other patrons at the swanky Melbourne restaurant. If he wasn't people watching, then he was glancing at his mobile phone, which sat on the table beside him. Though no new messages had announced themselves with the familiar buzzing of vibration, Cal couldn't help but check just in case. As he pressed a button, the smartphone's screen lit up revealing the text of his most recently received message.

Madison: *I tried, Cal. You know I'd love for you two to speak again. But I can't force her. I guess she still needs some time.*

It felt like the thousandth time he'd read over those words and each read had only aggravated him further. How could she possibly need more *time*? It had been fourteen long years, but it had felt like eons and he'd never once heard a word. Not one reply to a text message, an email or even a handwritten letter. In the beginning, he'd tried calling her old cell phone, then her parents' house, their high school friends, and even the university she'd left him to attend. But none of his efforts received any form of reply from her.

He'd even considered hiring a private investigator to track her down but hadn't, partly because his only connection to her—their mutual friend Madison—would never forgive him for it and, if for some crazy reason she did, he was certain that the-one-that-got-away wouldn't either. At any rate, he was lucky he still had Madison to turn to and that at least gave him some reassurance that the love of his life had actually existed and still lived somewhere out there in the world—waiting for him to find her.

"So, what do you think, Cal?" Natalie—no, Nadine—no, it was Natasha—gave him a wide grin. "Doesn't it sound incredible?"

Cal smiled half-heartedly and ran a hand through his shaggy, sandy blond hair. Though he didn't want to be rude and hated the fact that he might sound like an idiot if he said the wrong thing, he was also well aware that it was Friday and that the chances of his current woman-of-the-week making it beyond the weekend were slim to none.

"It sure does, Nat," he told her cheerfully. Surely, he would be safe with that moniker. *Nat* could pass for two of the potentials and if it really was Nadine, he'd just lie and say he'd known it all along.

"I know! Can you believe it?" his date asked him with a

smirk. "Me on the cover of a magazine!"

He offered her a wide, toothy grin. As he glanced over her, trying to reacquaint himself with the near stranger sitting before him, she covered his hand with hers.

It wasn't a surprise to hear her good news considering her appearance. She was a stunning blonde with a trim figure in a fitted gold mini-dress and had legs that any giraffe would be proud of. Her features were angular and exotic, perfect model material. But so were all his dates— his *weekly flings* as his favorite cousin Toby called them. She was only one in a sea of similarly beautiful creatures, but was still absolutely nothing in comparison to the-one-who-got-away.

"Where've you gone to?" The willowy being in front of him waved the fingers of her free hand beneath his nose.

"Um, sorry," Cal said, shaking himself free of his thoughts. "It's been a long week at work."

Nat smiled reassuringly and took both his hands in hers, clutching them affectionately on top of the table. "Don't worry, babe. I know a trick or two that might help relax you, but you'll have to wait until we get home."

As she winked at him, he forced a small smile in return. He'd clearly stayed with this one for too long. The use of *home* as a general term relating easily to each of their respective homes or any location where they both may reside at any one time terrified him almost as much as having his hands trapped within hers, forbidding him from checking his phone. Just the thought of it made him glance down once more.

"Are you waiting for a call?" Nat asked him, her expression becoming concerned.

He looked up at her and then slid his hands slowly free of hers, careful not to offend her. "No. It's probably just habit." Instinctively, his right hand reached for his smartphone and as if on cue, the screen lit up and the device began to vibrate with an incoming call.

Cal had a moment of elation at the thought that

perhaps this was the call he'd been waiting for, for over a decade. Maybe *she* had finally decided to contact him.

Yet, as he looked closer, the name "Jack" appeared and it became obvious that this was nothing more than a work call.

Cal glanced up at his date. Her happy expression had become perplexed.

"Sorry, but I've got to take this. It's work. It shouldn't take long."

Though her brows furrowed in disappointment, the corners of her mouth quirked upward as though in acknowledgement.

Content to escape her, even for a second, he nodded, put the cell phone to his ear and headed for the restaurant's reception area.

"What's happened?" he said once he'd pressed a button to answer the call.

"It's decided, Cal." Jack's deep voice sounded partially tinny. "The last of the board's anonymous votes have been counted. It seems they have voted *against* keeping the Gold Coast property."

Cal swore under his breath before realizing that the restaurant's hostess was watching him closely from the counter. Caught in her stare, she smirked at him flirtatiously. In an effort to hide his anger, Cal relaxed his firm expression and nodded kindly at her.

It was obvious that he had a natural charm with women. Besides the handsome features he'd received genetically and the brawny frame created after years of playing football, he also seemed to exude a certain magnetism. Tonight, even with his current date and in the creased grey business suit he'd worn all day, he'd still received numerous suggestive glances and one sneaky phone number. While it was mostly to his benefit, especially in obtaining his weekly flings, the extra attention could also be trying, especially when it occurred at the wrong time. This was definitely one of those times.

Struggling to maintain his composure at Jack's news, Cal watched carefully as the busty hostess returned his nod and forced her gaze back to the reservations diary on the countertop. Content that she was focused back on her duties, Cal turned away and headed closer to the far wall.

"Are you serious, Jack? Do they even care that it was my father's first property? Or that without that first success there would be no Hawthorne empire?"

Cal could hear Jack sigh through the phone.

"Cal, I know it meant a lot to you and your father, that you have many fond memories there, but it's been running at a loss for years now, eating through funds. The company would do much better to sell it, making a profit from the property location at the very least."

It was Cal's turn to sigh. He understood Jack was only trying to help. He had been his company's financial advisor—and his good friend—since before Cal's father had passed away four years ago and willed that Cal take over as CEO. Even the board of directors were only trying to do right by the company, right by him and his father's well-respected name. Although knowing they meant well afforded him some satisfaction, he didn't want to give up something so important to him without a solid fight. He had already lost the person with whom he'd imagined spending his entire future, so there was no way that he would easily lose the place that held the fondest memories of his past.

"When do they plan to sell?" Cal had to ask.

"Though it's not exactly a priority at the moment, it has been proposed that the property be put on the market in May."

"That's just over a month away," Cal spat. "That's too soon."

There was silence on the other end of the line before Jack spoke up once again. "It has to be done, Cal."

"What if—" Cal began, starting to pace along the wall. "What if they gave me the month? Let me do my best to resurrect the business, pique client interest and save the property. If I can turn things around and make the same weekly profit as our luxury resort in Sydney in the final week of the deal, then the property will stay in the company's portfolio? If not, it can go on the market the following week."

"Cal." Jack's tone was almost chiding.

"Come on, Jack," Cal said boldly. "Give me a chance. What would the company lose? I can use my own personal accounts to fund my pursuit and ask Liam to cover some of my prior commitments. Let me at least try."

Again, there was silence while Cal felt his palms grow sweaty. Besides getting in contact with his true love again, he'd never wanted anything more. He was certain that Liam—his amazing Chief Operating Officer—would be able to handle any important meetings that he may have to miss given the circumstances. Being a wealthy property tycoon in his own right also meant that his contributions to his beloved Gold Coast property wouldn't even come close to denting his extensive personal wealth. It was the perfect plan, if only he could secure the opportunity.

"It's a big ask," Jack said carefully. "Do you really think it's wise to aim for such a considerable profit?"

"I can do it, Jack."

There was a deep sigh through the electronic device.

"Very well, Cal. I'll run it by the board, but I believe there shouldn't be much opposition. As long as you pursue this yourself, using your own wealth and business smarts, I can see no problem. Just…," Jack paused warily.

"Yes?" Cal asked.

"Just don't be too disappointed if things don't go your way. You can't have everything you want, mate. Take solace in knowing that you gave your best effort to keep something you love."

Cal nodded automatically. His heart felt suddenly heavier, but he understood Jack's point. He stopped his pacing and his stare hardened. "Just as everyone should be innocent until proven guilty," he told him resolutely, "so shall I be optimistic about this task until it is proved impossible."

At Jack's kind farewell, Cal touched a button as he lowered the phone from his ear, ending the call.

He had one month to save the building in which he had spent the happiest days of his childhood. One month to prove to the board that it was worth the expense and that it could return a profit worthy of any of the businesses in the Hawthorne Incorporated's portfolio. He knew he could do it. He just needed some help.

After a few seconds of consideration, he walked over to the female receptionist behind the counter. As he approached, she glanced up and met his friendly gaze with a smile of her own.

"Can I help you?" Her voice was sweet, nearly flirtatious as she leaned toward him.

Cal exuded charm as his white smile widened. "Do you think you could do me a favor?"

He knew that what he had to ask wasn't entirely acceptable, but it was necessary. Natasha-Nadine-Natalie had overstayed her welcome in his life and it was time to cut her free. Besides, he had much more important things to do right now than return to the boredom of their so-called date. He just hoped she wouldn't make too much of a scene when the receptionist passed on the message that he had left without her. No, either way it would be fine. He would just leave a substantial tip in case she broke something valuable.

CHAPTER TWO

Lucy was dying or at least she was pretty sure she was. The stabbing pains in her head mixed with the rampant nausea in her gut were sure signs that her life was over. But there was also that incessant ringing as though she were beneath the huge brass bells in a church tower.

It took a long time for her to realize that the tune resembled that of her cell phone, just more thunderous, as though it was echoing loudly off the walls of a great cavern. She tried sitting up without much luck, so instead crawled on her belly, her short cotton pajama set stretching as she moved. Her eyes closed to the pain, she inched her way to the other side of the mattress.

At least she recognized where she was now. She'd somehow managed to make it back to her townhouse after last night. It was only supposed to have been a couple of drinks, something she hadn't had time for in ages. Her friends had insisted, almost begged her to come out with them, it had been so long. Then, at the discovery of her little secret, a few drinks had become a bender. Pausing, her head swimming, sickening dizziness consuming her, she wondered how she had let it get so bad?

Once she'd finally reached the side of the bed, she

stretched a slender arm over the edge, searching blindly for her leather handbag. Almost as soon as she'd found it, the ringing stopped.

"Damn it," she said, then immediately regretted it when her head boomed painfully with the sound of her own words.

She slumped further against the soft cushioning of the sheeted mattress until she felt as though the two had merged and she too, was now cushy softness. An instant of peaceful silence and stillness passed where she began to wonder if her rough night and subsequent hangover were just a karmic dream for her bad friendship skills, but then the ringing began again.

With a frustrated sigh, in which she became worried a little more might leave her lips than just her breath, she reached again for her phone. Once it was in her hand, she squinted open her eyes and clicked a button to answer the call. Realizing that she didn't have the strength to move her hand back to her ear, she switched the call to loudspeaker.

"Are you there? Lucy!" Steph's voice shrieked loudly, filling the bedroom and Lucy's head with sharp, stabbing sounds.

"Ugh. Steph." Lucy groaned before smooshing her face back into the soothing embrace of the mattress.

"Lucy? You sound really far away." Steph's tone became concerned.

Forcing herself to lift her heavy head and prop her chin on a nearby pillow, Lucy groaned. "How are you awake? And how are you not dead?"

"What? Oh, last night. You really should go drinking with us more often, Luce. You're really out of practice."

Steph's laughter seemed to pound through Lucy's eardrums like the rhythmic thump of a subwoofer. Lucy groaned in agony.

"What do you want? Tell me already so I can hang up and go back to bed."

"Rude, much?" Steph laughed again. "Okay, I'll tell you."

Lucy listened as Steph suddenly paused. She couldn't tell if she was struggling to find the right words, trying to build anticipation, or if she was about to give her some terrible news, but either way she wanted it over and done with—and over and done with now.

"Steph," Lucy almost pleaded.

"So, I got a call from Julia this morning."

Lucy frowned. Though her head wasn't quite screwed on straight at the current moment, alcohol having potentially fried around ninety percent of her brain cells, she was at the very least sure it was Saturday. And this Saturday, she was sure again, had not been a calendared working day, which then begged the question why had Julia—their boss—called Steph at all, unless she wanted tips on how to drink like a fish and not be affected the morning after.

"She tried calling you first, Luce, but you were dead to the world after last night, so then she called me. She's probably on the phone to Trent now too."

Though she was hearing everything in a sort of cotton-wool haze—her mind taking longer to process Steph's words—Lucy still managed to understand why Steph felt the need to clarify the sequence of calls. As the three executive managers of the company, Lucy, Steph, and Trent usually worked separately. Their own teams were given individual projects to bring to fruition and were rarely included in one another's work. That was, unless the job was extraordinarily large, or they were given the opportunity to compete for a project they desired.

"We have a big client coming in on Monday." Steph chuckled. "Did I say big? I meant huge! Even Julia is excited. She's asked us to come in a couple of hours early so that she can prep us. She didn't even want to say his name over the phone!" Steph laughed excitedly.

"He must be a big deal," Lucy said blandly.

Though this type of news would normally thrill her, the hangover was making it a struggle just to make it through the rest of the conversation without vomiting.

"Wow! You must be suffering," Steph said with astonishment.

A groan was all Lucy mustered in reply.

"Okay. I'll leave you be and call you again this afternoon. It's seriously exciting though, Luce! I wonder who he could be?"

Lucy felt another groan grumble out through her lips.

Steph sighed. "Okay, I'm going. Now, remember to hydrate and eat a serious breakfast." She laughed. "Or lunch, in your case. Talk to you later."

Lucy didn't answer, but pressed a button to end the call. As she did so, she noticed the time on the brightly lit screen. It was almost eleven. She hadn't slept that late in years.

Grumbling indiscernibly to herself, Lucy dropped her smartphone to the floor. She was never drinking again, she promised.

Still unable to lift herself up without the pollution in her gut threatening to expel itself, she clawed her way up higher on the mattress instead, keeping her body flush against the sheet. Only when she was a little more parallel with the lengthways of the bed, looked a little more like a normal sleeping form, did she finally stop her efforts and relax. It may have been almost eleven in the morning and much later than she'd snoozed since university, but she didn't care. She'd be sleeping in until she felt alive again, however long that may be.

Closing her eyes, she tried to ignore the dizziness filling the darkness behind her lids and the sea-sickening nausea in her stomach. Instead, she thought of what Steph had told her.

We have a big client coming in on Monday… didn't want to say his name over the phone!

Even though all positive feelings had left her because

she was clearly still dying—or at least felt like it—Lucy knew that way down, somewhere inside herself, she was excited. How could she not be? She loved her job and enjoyed all new projects, but one with extensive funding and a high-profile client often offered more opportunity for creativity and recognition.

She smiled at the thought, but even that movement seemed to hurt. Her brief smile faded and became a pouty frown. She was *definitely* never drinking again.

***

Cal had a clear view of the front door from where he lounged on a sofa in the popular St. Kilda cocktail bar. Being mid-afternoon and a Sunday meant that the intimate room was already becoming crowded.

Although he had been trying to wait patiently, having eagerly arrived half an hour early, he was unable to stop his foot from tapping on the polished wooden floor. Leaning toward the large glass coffee table between his sofa and the next, he pressed a button on his mobile phone to view the time. Madison was two minutes late.

His long fingers picked up the rhythm of his foot and began tapping on the edge of the sofa's cushioned arm.

"Can I get you another?"

Cal had been too distracted by his own thoughts to notice the willowy waitress appear beside him. Though she had trendy black-rimmed glasses and a colorful sleeve tattoo, her cheeky smile had him wondering whether it was time for him to change his usual type of woman for his weekly fling.

"Ah, no." He grinned and then motioned to the empty scotch glass. "I'm confident we'll order more when my friend arrives."

The waitress nodded and Cal watched her walk over to an adjacent table, his gaze firmly planted on the swish of her hips as she did so.

"Still on the prowl, I see."

Cal turned to see Madison Foley standing in front of him, a manicured hand on the jeans that hugged her narrow hips and a smirk teasing her lips.

"You know I wouldn't have to be," Cal said as he stood to greet her, "if you'd just give me *her* number."

Madison laughed heartily and then reached her arms wide to embrace him, her beige jacket opening to reveal a black lace camisole. Cal returned her hug affectionately, noting that her tall, lanky frame hadn't changed much in the many years he'd known her. As she released him from their embrace and stepped back to take a seat on the opposite sofa, Cal did the same and gazed over her familiar features.

When they were at school together, Madison had always been heavily into sports. A tomboy at heart, she was even passionate about the rougher sports like hockey and rugby. She'd always had a messy ponytail and a skinned knee, but these days her interests had changed dramatically. After eloping with Robert six years ago, she'd channeled her love of sport into hobbies they could do together. Her tanned skin and sun-kissed strawberry blonde hair told him she was still an avid surfer, but her French tipped false fingernails made it obvious she was taking a break from rock climbing. While her round face and kind hazel eyes were attractive, she had never been anything more to him than a close friend and quasi-sister.

"You look tired," she told him. Her eyes narrowed on his features and she appeared to study him closely.

"Work has been more stressful of late."

Madison crossed her legs and relaxed further into the sofa. "You need a holiday."

Cal shrugged. "One day."

He smiled at her then, all pearly white and charming and it only took a second for her stare to become suspicious.

"Okay, out with it," she told him. "What are you

offering me this time?"

Annoyed that his charm didn't seem to work on her, Cal sighed defeatedly. "Once a month we catch up, sometimes even twice, and every time I ask you the same question, but you never give me a good enough answer."

Madison rolled her eyes at him. "The answer is good enough. It's the outcome it offers you that isn't."

"Why can't you just give me her number? An email address? Something?" Cal huffed and crossed his arms over his muscular chest, crinkling the soft material of his black V-neck sweater.

Folding her hands in her lap, Madison's expression became more serious, almost chiding. "I know it's been many years, Cal and that you miss her terribly, but you know that I can't just give you her new phone number without her permission."

Cal leaned forward eagerly. "Why not? I know how much you wish we were all close again, like we were at school. How could it hurt?"

"She could never speak to me again," Madison scoffed. "You might've been able to survive more than a decade with the cold shoulder from her, but I couldn't. She's like family to me. You both are." Madison sighed. "You'll just have to wait until she's ready."

A frustrated growl escaped his lips, and he threw himself back into the sofa. "And how many more years will that be? I miss her. I can't stand living without her."

Sitting forward in her chair, Madison snatched Cal's left hand from where it gripped his dark-jean-clad knee and then held it reassuringly in her own. Her hazel gaze bore into his smoky-blue eyes and her expression became painfully sympathetic.

"Have faith that it will all work out," she begged him. "I know she still cares for you, deep down beneath the pain and the anger."

He shook his head in exasperation. "But how did I hurt her? Why is she so furious with me? Can't you tell me that?"

Sounding solemn, Madison sighed. "I can only tell you what I always tell you, that your behavior in high school had her doubting the sincerity of your relationship together and that she needs you to understand how badly you hurt her before she can forgive you. Unfortunately, I'd be breaking a promise to her if I told you anything more."

"Damn you both and your girly pinky-swears," Cal teased half-heartedly.

As he gently released his hand from hers, he gave her a small smile. A moment of stoic silence passed between them before Cal narrowed his gaze, his brows furrowed in consideration.

"Well then, before I ask you how much Rob's enjoying his new jet ski, perhaps you can do me a different favor?"

"I'm listening." Madison's expression filled with careful curiosity.

"Since you haven't given me what I really wanted, I think—at the very least—I deserve to see a recent picture of her."

Madison chuckled and reached for her smartphone. "On that, I'd be happy to oblige."

***

Her reflection in the mirrored walls of the elevator made Lucy smile. It had been a glorious morning so far. She had woken early in her Fitzroy townhouse, cheerful enough to take a run through the nearby Carlton Gardens before preparing herself for the excitement of the working day. As well as ensuring her long chocolate bob was blow-dried neatly, she'd also spent more time than she could ever remember fussing over the perfection of her make-up.

Though Lucy had resigned herself to the fact that she would always be of an average height and have a mostly average figure, she was grateful that her facial features resembled her mother's. Her scarlet lipstick covered plump lips and was bright against the perfect paleness of her English rose skin. Her big, tranquil blue eyes were framed by large, dark eyelashes and seemed to glow beneath the smoky eyeshadow. With her red and ivory silk blouse, the tight black pencil skirt that finished a few inches above the knee, her shiny black pumps and matching petite shoulder bag, she felt ready for anything.

Lucy was glad it was Monday. She was happy she hadn't heard anything more from Maddy over the weekend and that she'd survived her hangover from Friday night. She was also excited to be on the verge of a new project, but most of all, she was thrilled to be going to work. It wasn't something she told herself daily, yet she couldn't help but feel—at least the majority of the time—that she was one of those lucky people who had managed to find a career that strongly incorporated her passion.

She loved understanding niche markets and finding clever ways to seduce even the stingiest people to spend their money on fantastic and lovely things. She never looked at it as manipulating or cheating people out of their hard-earned money, because that had never been her style. She would leave that darker form of advertising to Trent and his team. Instead, Lucy saw what she did as a way to tap into the customer's very soul, her ingenious techniques only a tool able to captivate the deepest desires in an individual. Lucy believed that the seduction of her marketing methods was one of true love where she helped customer and product unite.

A vaguely feminine, automated voice in the elevator announced her arrival at the twelfth floor, snapping Lucy free of her thoughts. Turning away from the mirrored wall as the elevator doors opened, Lucy's smile widened. *Here we go*, she thought.

On the wall above the tall reception desk was an elaborate ebony, yellow, and emerald sign emblazoned with the words *Insight Marketing*. Stepping from the elevator, Lucy headed past the desk and the smiling young woman who sat behind it wearing a sapphire silk blouse and a blonde ponytail.

"Morning, Mia," Lucy said cheerfully.

"You're in a fabulous mood this morning, Lucy." Grinning, Mia stood and smoothed her floral skirt as she hurried from behind the reception desk to grab Lucy as she passed. "Sorry, I couldn't make it for drinks after work the other evening. Steph must have told you my little sister, Vicki, was in town?"

Lucy paused in her stride. "All good." She smiled with a light-hearted shrug. "We'll have to do it again sometime, as long as there's a three-drink limit for me."

Mia spat out a laugh. "Steph told me how *wonderful* you felt the next day," she said mockingly.

Rolling her eyes, Lucy's expression contorted in disgust. "Never again."

"Whatever you say." Mia's smirk was almost mischievous, then she gestured down the open corridor before them. "I thought you'd like to know that our mystery client is in the boardroom with Julia." Her eyes were wide with curiosity. "They've already been in there for half an hour."

Surprised, Lucy frowned in concern. "I thought she'd wanted us in early to discuss tactics before the client arrived?"

Mia shrugged. "Apparently, he was very eager to get started. He was already waiting downstairs when Julia and I arrived at seven to open up."

Shocked by Mia's news, Lucy's eyebrows quirked. "You've seen him then?"

Nodding, Mia's gaze drifted toward the direction of the boardroom, which still lay just out of sight beyond the expanse of empty, brightly colored office cubicles and the line of glass-doored offices. Following her gaze, Lucy nibbled at her lower lip.

Her excitement at the project and the mysteriousness

of the new client had overshadowed her nerves until now. Who was this enthusiastic client, so eminent and affluent that Julia had thought it best not to divulge his name over the phone? The secrecy was both exhilarating and terrifying. She wondered just how much longer she'd have to stay in the dark.

"Let's just say," Mia began, drawing Lucy's gaze back to her, "that you won't find it difficult to spend a little extra time with this one. If I could, I'd volunteer to be around him twenty-four-seven."

Lucy smirked briefly, but then her eyebrows furrowed. It wasn't odd for them to have a very attractive male client, although they were usually already married or searching for a lover of the male persuasion, but it was definitely rare for them to have a male client that had even Mia—Steph's girlfriend—reconsidering her sexuality.

"Thanks for the heads up," Lucy told her with an appreciative smile. Then she nodded in the direction of the boardroom. "Do you know if Julia wants us to join her in there or wait until they're finished?"

Mia raised a hand and pointed her index finger toward one of the glass-doored offices. "Steph's in her office waiting for Julia's okay, but Trent hasn't come in yet. When you're all here, I'll call through and let her know."

Giving her a wink, Mia headed back behind the reception desk and Lucy continued down the wide aisle.

At Steph's open office door, Lucy paused and glanced in at her colleague who looked uncharacteristically professional in her graphite-colored tailored suit as she stared intensely at her computer.

"All good, Steph?"

Steph glanced up from the screen as Lucy stepped inside. With a smile, she waved a hand toward the monitor.

"Just checking the leave calendar. It's our third anniversary in July. Mia loves air travel, so I thought we could catch a flight somewhere nice."

As she leaned casually on the chair in front of Steph's

desk, Lucy's amused smile turned sly. "Planning anything special then? Three years is a long time."

Steph narrowed her gaze innocently. "I'm not sure what you mean."

Lucy chuckled.

"And what about you, Luce? You never take leave. Surely a holiday would do you good?"

"I live to work." Lucy shrugged. "I know it's boring, but it makes me happy."

"I think it makes you insane," Steph said as she stood and walked around to the front of her desk. "You need a love life."

Lucy rolled her eyes. "I have a love life, thank you very much. I love my family, I love you, I love Mia, I love Rosie, I love Maddy, and sometimes I think I could even love Julia."

"Now that is insane," Steph scoffed.

The distant sound of Mia's voice calling out interrupted their shared laughter.

"Trent's here."

As Steph and Lucy exited the office, they saw Trent striding toward them. His tall, taut figure fit into flawlessly pressed black slacks, which matched his impeccably ironed salmon suit shirt and his perfectly preened black hair. From a short distance, Lucy could admire the fact that Trent was good-looking, although his features were possibly a little too angular. It was only when he got closer and you had to deal with the real human man that he became less attractive.

"Have we seen the *piggybank* yet?"

Trent always referred to their wealthier clients as piggybanks, claiming that he could *smash* them open with his extraordinary marketing ideas and that the money would just keep pouring out.

"Don't let Julia hear you call him that," Steph warned.

Trent shrugged.

"No," Lucy answered, wary of the glare her colleagues

shared. "We haven't yet had the pleasure."

The quick clip-clop of high heels had all three turning to look toward the reception desk. Mia was almost running toward them, pointing a finger in the direction of the boardroom as she did so.

"They're coming out," she said, excitement making her voice shrill.

As Mia joined them, all four began to stare down the empty aisle, as though their keen expressions alone were enough to will Julia and their new client into view.

Seconds passed, an eternity of time in what felt like deafening silence. It was only when Julia's girlish giggle echoed in the quiet space around them that Lucy realized she'd been holding her breath in anticipation. Steph and Mia seemed to share a look of confusion at the feminine sound.

"Is that Julia?" Steph asked in a whisper.

In wide-eyed surprise, Mia nodded.

A door closed with a thud and two sets of footsteps thumped almost in unison. As they grew louder, Julia appeared. She walked confidently into sight in her grey asymmetrical dress, her black micro bob and straight fringe barely shifting with the movement of her stride. Then a navy-suited leg stretched around the corner, followed by the rest of the man himself. And Lucy began to have a panic attack.

"What a honey," purred Mia, while Steph rolled her eyes.

Lucy clutched a hand to her pounding heart, convinced that it was the only way to keep it from bursting through her chest.

What was he doing here?

She felt faint. Thoughts whirled around in her mind, making it difficult to focus on any one. She should've been angry, furious even, but instead she was terrified. She had to get out of there, away from him—now.

Stiff as a statue, she forced herself to look at Steph.

"You know that holiday you wanted me to take?" she told her. "Well, I'm taking it now. Bye."

Steph, Mia, and Trent stood confused, watching when Lucy turned away from them and headed for the elevator. Then, their new client spoke.

"Lucy!" The rich male voice echoed through the open room. It was deep, almost sensual and filled with a kind of desperation.

The sound was enough to force three sets of wide eyes back to stare at the sinfully attractive, enigmatic man now standing next to Julia.

As Steph stared, a mental clog seemed to clink into place and her jaw dropped.

"Shut the front door," she breathed. "It's Lucy's *bome.*"

CHAPTER THREE

She'd literally taken his breath away.

Cal had hoped that when he first saw her, their first encounter in fourteen years, he would be perfectly suave. He'd hoped that he would exude some kind of incredible charm and she would see him, forget her reasons for abandoning him, and just run into his arms.

Instead, she had stolen his breath away and he, in turn, had turned her sweet, curious gaze into one of absolute fear. Her kissable crimson lips had formed a perfect "O" before she spun her sexy figure around and strode toward the entrance, her luscious backside swaying, mesmerizing him. A primal lust had swept over him, destroying all sensible thoughts for a moment. But it was an instant too long and she was almost to the elevator by the time he'd called out.

Though it had been sheer coincidence, fate he preferred to think, that had intervened and drawn him to her workplace, it was in fact at the insistence of the Hawthorne Incorporated's marketing team that he'd even considered doing business with the firm. They were the best of the best, he'd been told, a giant in the independent business scene. If he was going to revitalize the Gold

Coast property, draw vast numbers of new clientele, and make good on his side of the deal, then he needed the help of the people at Insight Marketing.

It hadn't been until late last night, while drowning his sorrows in a bottle of bourbon after his fruitless meeting with Madison, that he'd decided to ask for the internet's opinion of the firm. After a few clicks in, he'd found her and needed to pinch himself to prove he hadn't been dreaming, hadn't fallen into some kind of alcoholic coma.

He'd found her. He'd really finally found *his* Lucy Spencer.

Cal had barely slept through the night, fearful that she would somehow sense his discovery, that she would abandon him once again. He'd kept the knowledge to himself, grateful that he hadn't told Madison the name of the marketing firm he'd be working with. It had made him almost paranoid that even the smallest utterance of the discovery would somehow work against him and she would disappear. He hadn't even said it out loud to himself.

Cal couldn't believe how close she'd been, how nearby she'd worked for so many years, without him even running into her in the city. It was exhilarating, shiver-inducingly strange to think that she could've passed him on the street numerous times and they'd just missed each other by a side of the street, by a corner, by a glance. With this new knowledge, Cal could've almost felt certain that the universe had been trying to keep them apart, had it not been for the fact that he'd finally found her.

Being so close to something he'd wanted for such a long period of time had made him desperately apprehensive and tense. Unable to sleep and with the fear and the constant waiting grating on him, he'd arrived two hours early to his meeting with the Insight Marketing team.

Though Cal had planned to catch Lucy in the lobby as she'd arrived, hoping that they might have some privacy during their reunion, he'd been unlucky enough to have been discovered by the director of the firm as he'd paced nervously around the decorative lounge.

Agreeing to her request, he'd come upstairs and mentally altered his plan. Surely, if he was already in the office, it would make things easier. For one, there would be no chance of Lucy spotting him through the glass entrance as her boss had—pacing around in the lobby like a nutter—giving her an opportunity to run away before he'd even seen her. And secondly, she wouldn't be able to escape so easily from the twelfth floor, not when her boss and work colleagues were around, making it necessary for her to go through the difficulty of explaining herself if she wished to leave.

Though it had been a good plan in theory, he'd severely underestimated her—and her lingering hostile feelings toward him.

The bell of the elevator had already rung by the time his wits finally returned. Lucy was now completely out of sight and her three colleagues were still standing in front of him, halfway between him and the elevator, looking as stunned by the situation as he'd been just a moment before.

Apologizing to the striking older woman beside him— whose name he'd been unable to put to memory due to his intense distress—he began to jog down the aisle past colorful cubicles and glass-doored offices. With another apology, he pushed through the three staff members, hindered only slightly by the male who—protectively or possibly jealously—tried to block his path.

Cal was a few feet from the elevator as the doors locked in place and the light of the large down arrow on the wall blinked off. Lunging at the buttons, his first instinct was to call the second lift so that he could follow her down. Yet, when he glanced around the small elevator foyer, a large door to the right caught his attention. *Fire door*, it read.

He ran over to it, tried the handle and the door opened inwardly. Relieved that he hadn't set off an alarm, Cal dashed inside and began hurrying down the concrete steps. He managed to descend each set in gigantic leaps, taking three steps at a time, sometimes five and the big, black numbers on the fire doors on each second landing were changing, falling. He was at floor ten, then nine. Cal moved faster. Seven. Before he knew it, he was at floor five, then four. Almost there. He knew he would beat her to the lobby. He had to—there was no alternative. He had to see her again—and this time, she wouldn't be able to get away.

*

Lucy had been forced to stop at three floors, even though she'd pressed the *doors closed* button with such force she'd expected to break it. People had come and gone and stayed, but she was now on her way to ground level.

Ignoring the whispers of the two young businessmen behind her, Lucy stepped closer to the elevator door, anxiously waiting for it to open into the tall, white tiled expanse of the lobby.

She couldn't believe Callum had found her! If she wasn't certain that she'd scream the whole time, Lucy would've called Maddy and told her off for her betrayal. How else could Cal have known where she'd worked? He hadn't even looked surprised—or at least not initially. Once he'd seen her fear, she'd noticed his expression change and his eyes begin to grow large with shock. How surprised he must have been when she'd turned and left!

But, what had he expected her to do? Run into his arms? How ridiculous!

At least she'd managed to have enough sense to get away, even though fear had all but paralyzed her. But what was she to do now? Cal knew where she worked. She might have escaped him this time, might be able to avoid his calls to her work phone, ignore the emails to her work account, but that didn't change the fact that he knew where she'd be five days a week. It also wouldn't stop him from dropping by the office whenever he wanted, making her life miserable in the process. She couldn't work from home every day.

A thought flashed into Lucy's mind, the image of Julia's displeased expression as she'd turned to leave. Biting her lower lip, Lucy wrung her hands nervously. That was assuming she still had a job after today.

As her apprehension built at the thought of losing the job she loved so dearly, a sickening feeling of dread washed over her. She was trapped either way. If Julia didn't fire her for her poor behavior in front of an important client, then she had no doubt that Cal would be there, daily if necessary, trying to convince her of the sincerity of their friendship. If Julia did choose to cease her employment with the firm, then he could easily get her details from Trent or anyone else with unscrupulous morals when offered a great deal of money. Lucy thought even Julia would cave if seduced by the promise of further business dealings.

That was it then. She was trapped and it was over. After more than a decade of trying to move on from the past, it had finally, and literally, caught up with her.

No, she thought defiantly. *I will not give in to that liar... that womanizer... that false friend!*

While she still had her free will and while she still remembered the toxicity of their past relationship, she was not about to give in to his request for friendship so easily. He had betrayed her. He had hurt her. He had broken her heart. In her mind, she couldn't see any coming back from that. What they'd had, the relationship they'd shared, was over and always would be. He was wasting his time if he believed that they could be anything more than passing acquaintances now.

Having talked herself out of a panic attack, Lucy raised her head high and squared her shoulders, confident in her convictions. She wasn't that pathetic teenager anymore, wasn't innocent and malleable and naïve. She was a strong, intelligent, sensible woman and she would fight Cal off until he finally left her alone.

"Ground floor."

The sound of the elevator's automated voice had Lucy's heart leaping. She was almost free, at least for today, and that at any rate would garner her more time to plan what to do next.

As the doors opened slowly, Lucy began to squeeze herself through the small, but widening opening. She wasn't about to waste any time waiting for useless things like elevator doors, especially when Cal may have followed her down and could be in the other lift behind her. She couldn't risk even an extra second.

That thought had Lucy looking briefly over her shoulder at the lift as she stepped free of the confinement of the elevator and into the clean, quiet lobby. Distracted, she slammed straight into the hard body of some tall, innocent bystander. As she reeled back, her hand pressed against the very muscular, masculine figure beneath the soft suit jacket. She began to apologize. It was only when she turned her head, her eye-level meeting the dark navy of his suit collar and the crisp white of his shirt, that her stomach sank. Pushing herself away from him, Lucy's gaze rose up along the line of a honey-tanned neck, beyond a strong jaw roughened with sandy colored stubble to that all too familiar face.

Though many years had passed and they were now both thirty-two, Callum Hawthorne was still as ruggedly handsome as ever. The almost military short haircut she remembered him being fond of during their school days had been replaced with a modern style, trimmed close at the back and sides with a neatly styled mop of sandy blond hair on top. His honey-hued skin, with a slight flush around his cheeks still looked delectable with just the slightest of creases around his full, cupid's bow lips and at the corners of his alluring blue-grey eyes. Yet those eyes, she observed, no longer held that teasing glint that always made her smile, but were instead full of a desperation and longing she had never seen in them before.

It had been no more than a mere second, maybe two, before Lucy realized that she had paused in her retreat, absolutely captivated by him. She was glad it was early enough that the expanse of the white-tiled lobby was almost empty of people and that her moment of stupidity could pass almost unnoticed. Mentally chiding herself, she backed up and felt her eyes grow wide as she began to feel more and more like a cornered animal. But it was too late. As she moved back, his hand shot out and grabbed her wrist.

"Lucy."

He'd said her name with such pleading despair, that the hand she'd involuntarily begun to raise to slap him paused in its motion. She stared deeply into his smoky-blue eyes, enthralled by the emotion in his voice. Then he pulled her, forcing her to stumble toward him and the movement snapped her back to reality. The palm of her hand hit his face with an audible whack.

"How dare you!" she growled at him as she tried to release herself from his grip.

But her struggle was futile. He was simply too strong and his hand, large as it was, wrapped wholly around her wrist with ease. As her free hand, still sore from where it had slapped against his cheek, fell to her side, his free hand in turn went to his reddened skin. Shock filled his gorgeous eyes as he gazed down at her.

"How dare I?" Cal spoke the words slowly, his voice full of incredulity.

Lucy felt fury contort her expression. Angrily, she poked his hard chest with her index finger.

"Yes, you! How dare you come here and interfere with my work? Who knows if I even have a job after the display upstairs? How could you do that to me?"

With rage and adrenalin filling her veins, Lucy felt her

body tremble slightly. Her heart ached with the fear of losing her beloved job, but she knew a deeper fear existed. As she felt her face blush hotly and her eyes begin to well with tears, she looked away from him and tried to regain her composure. She would not cry in front of him, she wouldn't give him that pleasure.

Yet, she knew deep down why she was really upset, why she was really terrified. The thought of giving in, of letting Cal back into her heart again was much more frightening than losing even the most perfect job in the world. For she was certain, if she opened herself up to him, gave him everything he wanted, then he would surely break her heart all over again.

Clenching her hands into fists, she fought for control over her emotions and then glared back up at Cal. The jovial expression she was so used to seeing on a younger version of that face was non-existent and replaced by a mixture of confusion and compassion. With his furrowed brows shadowing his eyes and his sensuous lips poised open as if ready to protest, he looked like a beaten puppy and her heart ached to make that kissable mouth smile again.

Damn it, Lucy thought angrily as she forced her eyes to the floor.

That one instant had proved it all, and it was worse than she'd imagined. Somewhere inside that treasonous organ, the one that used to skip a beat every time Cal had winked at her teenage self, there was a piece of her that had never truly given up on him. It was as though the love she'd had for him was branded inside her forever, both a permanent reminder and a permanent weakness. And that, she was sure, was definitely the most terrifying thing of all.

*

Cal could barely breathe, even though his mouth hung open ready to either retort or apologize. He just couldn't seem to decide which.

How dare he, Lucy had said, and she'd been right, in part.

Her shocked reaction to his being there could be enough to jeopardize her employment, which would explain her fear and the tears he'd watched her struggle to contain. Yet, that was something he was almost certain he could guarantee wouldn't happen. With his wealth and influence, nothing was ever too far out of reach, especially ensuring a very clever marketing professional stayed put in her very successful marketing job.

From where he held tightly onto her delicate, pale wrist, Cal began to caress Lucy's skin reassuringly with his fingers.

"I would never do that to you," he told her, his voice deepening with sincerity. "I would never do anything to jeopardize your livelihood. Madison has told me how much you love your job."

On hearing Madison's name, Lucy's gaze rose back to his, and he found himself drowning in the depths of her tranquil blue eyes. It was like staring into the idyllic waters surrounding a tropical island, all beautiful bright blue and turquoise hues. If he'd been paying more attention, he would have realized that they were filled with a fierce fury, which only seemed to be growing as each millisecond passed. But he was oblivious and—like a love-starved pet—he was completely mesmerized.

"Maddy told you," Lucy seethed through gritted teeth.

Cal nodded obediently. "I always ask her about you."

It only took an instant for the ferociousness in her eyes to spread across her face.

"I knew it," she all but screamed.

Cal was flabbergasted. What had happened? What had he missed?

Then, distracted by her outburst, he made another mistake and his grip on Lucy's wrist loosened slightly. As if sensing his lapse in control, she used the whole weight of her small frame to jerk herself free of his hold and with a triumphant sigh she began to back away.

"So, you orchestrated this together, did you? What, did

you seduce Maddy too? Why can't you just leave me alone?"

Cal's gaze narrowed with concern. "What are you talking about, Luce?"

Worried that she'd run before he had a chance to explain, Cal reached out and took a step toward her. But, Lucy immediately backed farther away, taking two steps for his single stride.

"What did you give her to make her finally tell you where I was?"

Her fiery glare was enough to make his fingers ache to touch her, to soothe her. He hated seeing her in so much distress.

"Nothing." His voice was calm, pacifying. "She didn't tell me."

Lucy frowned and her gaze dropped from his, confusion clearly clouding her expression.

"But I—" She shook her head with irritation and glanced back up at him. "But how did you know that I'd be here?"

Cal smiled as he remembered the moment of pure serendipity, the second he'd seen her gorgeous face on the team's profile page on the Insight Marketing website. *Executive Manager Lucy S.*, it had read. Cal had tried searching the internet for her before, but to no avail. There had always been too many Lucy Spencers and he'd been convinced that she must have altered her name. Yet, this time he'd found her, so simply found her, as though the universe had finally pointed her out to him.

"Fate," he said confidently.

When her uncertain expression refused to waver, he shrugged nonchalantly.

"Maybe luck, coincidence even. My marketing team referred me to your firm regarding a new project I'm working on."

Lucy's eyes narrowed suspiciously, but she didn't back away as Cal took another careful step toward her in an attempt to close the painful distance.

"It was only last night that I found out you happened to work for the same firm. I haven't even told Madison what I discovered. I didn't want to jinx anything, risk you finding out I was coming and then not giving me a chance to explain."

Crossing her arms over her ample chest, Lucy's gaze roamed over Cal's face, as though assessing his expression would help her recognize his honesty.

Although he tried to fight the urge, Cal's eyes slipped down, roaming over the full, pert breasts that were being further thrust in his direction above the silky fabric of Lucy's blouse with each shallow breath. As he imagined gently nibbling that plump, creamy skin between his teeth, he felt an ache of longing in his groin.

"What makes you think you even deserve a chance to explain?" Lucy's voice was soft and to the point, sounding very much as though she was testing him.

Cal looked up into Lucy's wary eyes. "Because I care about you. Because I miss you and I'm pretty sure you've missed me too."

Lucy's full, crimson lips morphed from a defiant pout into a firm line. "That's it? Because you missed me?"

As a spark of white, hot anger flickered through her spectacular turquoise eyes, Cal felt himself swallow nervously.

"Yes." He nodded slowly. "My life has been empty without you in it, Luce. I just want things to go back to the way they were."

It was a lie and Cal knew it, but he was too afraid that the truth would only prove to scare her off quicker.

"The way they were," she repeated, her tone slightly incredulous.

Feeling suddenly overwhelmingly anxious, Cal moved closer to her in an effort to close the remaining gap of agonizing space between them. But Lucy was too quick for him this time and backed up, putting even more distance between them than they'd had just a moment before.

He sighed, paused in place, and nodded at her. "Yes. Like it was before. Is that too much to ask?"

"Hmm," she said as her index finger went to her lips and she appeared to pretend to think for a second. "Is it?" Her tone was abruptly sarcastic. Then her furious gaze bore into him. "Yes, I think it is," she told him. She pointed her index finger aggressively in his direction, but was careful to keep at a safe distance. "Of course, *you* would like to go back to that, wouldn't you? What, aren't there enough women left in your hemisphere of wealth and success that you've got to come trolling down into mine?"

Cal's jaw dropped in astonishment. How had they gotten onto this subject? Having her back in his life and his crazy dating habits were definitely not the same thing, even though *dating* and *her* would make a fine topic all on its own.

Quickly, he shook his head. He had to clear up the misunderstanding, even if he hadn't a clue as to how it had happened. Was this why she'd refused to reconnect with him sooner? His terrible dating behavior? What had Madison told her?

"No, Luce. You've got it wrong." Cal opened his mouth to continue, but she shut him down.

"Don't you dare call me that! I am not *your Luce* anymore! And I'll never be that same person to you again!"

Her words struck him like an arrow through the heart and he felt himself reach for her once more, wounded but desperate.

Dismissing his gesture, she spun around and walked away swiftly, nearly running toward the front doors of the building's elaborate facade.

"Lucy!" Cal called after her, but he knew she wouldn't stop. He'd really done it this time, though he'd had no idea what he'd done.

She needs you to understand how badly you hurt her before she can forgive you.

Madison's words rang in his ears. Yet it still didn't help him understand.

Obviously, he had to have done something terrible, something wicked enough for Lucy to prefer keeping him out of her life for good rather than face dealing with him and what he'd done on a daily basis. But what was it? Was he more of an obnoxious, self-centered bastard than he thought he was? Or was he just completely stupid, ignorant, and oblivious to the pain he'd caused her?

Cal stared after her, his mind racing, trying to discover the reason behind her anger toward him. Then, as he watched, Lucy disappeared out the door like an angel in a ray of bright, white sunlight. *His angel.*

And Cal suddenly knew what he had to do. One way or another, Lucy was going to tell him what he had done to hurt her so badly and then, he would do anything and everything in his power to make things right before he told her how he truly felt about her.

Then, he vowed to himself, *I'll never ever do anything to lose her again.*

CHAPTER FOUR

The sun had set about an hour ago and Lucy still hadn't turned the lights on in her townhouse. From where she sat cross-legged in her spandex gym gear on her burgundy sofa, she could see through the glass sliding door and out over her balcony into the moonlit night. Streetlights brightened the tree-lined paths and glowed over the dark road, while the lights inside the adjacent houses and units led the curious eyes of any voyeur into the depths of a stranger's home.

It was the flickering colors of the television that drew Lucy's gaze back onto the mindless reality series. She'd been forced to switch it on once she'd realized it was going to take a whole lot more than the usual to get over what had happened that day. As well as having suffered through a last-minute kick-boxing class, she had already eaten a whole sickening pint of Pina Colada flavored sorbet and spent a budget-obliterating amount of money online on those two dresses she thought absolutely too extravagant for any realistic occasion. Yet, so far, nothing was working. Even her go-to television show, which always seemed to put her in a good mood or at least clear her thoughts of any difficult issues, was letting her down.

As the second couple of budding entrepreneurs in this episode tried to sell their business ideas to the five critical, shark-like industry titans, Lucy found herself getting an itchy finger on the television's remote.

That proved it, she thought to herself with irritation. *Clearly nothing can help me relax.*

She was considering switching off the traitorous show and heading to the all-night pharmacy on the corner to buy sleeping pills to aid her sleep when she heard the doorbell chime. Warily, she forced herself off the sofa and out of the room, toward her front door. After checking through the peephole and seeing a waving Steph and smiling Mia, Lucy unlocked the door. It was only as she opened it and the bright glow of the streetlamps scalded her night vision, that she realized she'd should've turned on the lights in her townhouse as she went, giving her eyes a chance to adjust beforehand. Yet, she had been too lazy to pull herself up from the couch before and too busy sulking, annoyed that she couldn't improve her mood, to bother to turn on the lights once she'd gotten up.

"You're in a bad way," Steph said worriedly, as she glanced over Lucy's sweat-stained gym attire and then back up into her squinting eyes.

"Well, she has just survived the reunion from hell," explained Mia as she pushed past Steph to hug Lucy tightly. "We're here for you, hon."

As the wool from Mia's lilac cardigan tickled her nose, Lucy frowned helplessly at Steph from where her head was propped on her girlfriend's shoulder. But, all Steph could do was smile. Then, as quickly as the embrace began, it ended and Mia started off down the hallway toward the kitchen, her brown boots thudding on the bare floorboards.

"Where are your fancy glasses?" Mia threw the question almost rhetorically over her shoulder.

"We brought wine." Cheerfully, Steph lifted a lumpy canvas bag from where it had hung low next to her faded jeans and revealed the necks of a couple of dark bottles.

"And chocolate," Mia added, sticking her head out of the now well-lit kitchen. "And we're ordering pizza."

Nodding, Steph pushed past Lucy and headed deeper into the townhouse, turning lights on as she went.

Lost in a mixture of surprise, annoyance and gratitude, Lucy watched her friend disappear into the kitchen.

"Make yourself at home," she said sarcastically to herself.

Then she turned, looking out into the peaceful night as the banging of cupboards rang out behind her and for a moment, just a brief moment, she considered that it might be safer for her out there in the dark than in the warmth of her own home.

With a frown and a deep, hopeless sigh, Lucy shut her front door.

***

Although her hair was still damp from the shower Mia had ordered her to take, Lucy slicked it back into a stubby ponytail. Having slipped into a pair of black lace-edged shorts and an oversized white t-shirt with a cartoon of a fox and a clever witticism on the front, Lucy felt suitably and casually dressed enough for the occasion. Now, she just hoped she was mentally prepared.

Realistically, she knew that, while Steph and Mia were here to offer her some emotional support, they were also here to tell her something big. Lucy was betting it was bad news. Either that she had been fired after her unprofessional display or worse, that she was being ordered back into work tomorrow to deal with their new huge-deal-of-a-client, Cal. With a resigned sigh, she made her way downstairs to the lounge room.

As she entered, Steph and Mia glanced up from where they'd made themselves at home on her large, L-shaped sofa.

"Smart as a—" Steph studied Lucy's shirt as she read and then she grinned. "Are you wearing that for our benefit or your own?"

Lucy shrugged solemnly and came to sit beside them. "I guess it's an armor of sorts."

Mia snorted out a giggle. "You're not going into battle, Luce. We're not here to fight."

Nodding, Lucy breathed. "I know."

Steph placed a hand on Lucy's bare knee reassuringly. "I hope you don't mind, but we've already ordered the pizzas. I know Mediterranean with extra cheese is your favorite."

"Thanks, Steph." Lucy covered Steph's hand with her own before gesturing at the television. "What are you watching?"

"Mia loves any romantic reality crap," Steph said as she removed her hand from Lucy's knee and then glanced back at the screen.

Mia hit Steph's shoulder playfully with the back of her hand. "Shut up. I've seen you get emotional when he has to decide which of the final two girls he should propose to."

Rolling her eyes mockingly at Mia, Steph then glanced back to Lucy. "Either way, it's not important now. We can switch it off if you like?"

Lucy was suddenly feeling apprehensive. Mia and Steph were staring at her with such concern and such attentiveness, it felt disturbing. She frowned at them, trying to show her displeasure.

"Should I bother to ask why or are you just going to come out with it?"

Steph and Mia shared a glance before returning to look at her again.

Taking a deep, steadying breath, Steph began. "Callum Hawthorne told Julia that he would only work with the firm if you were on board." She paused, her face contorting slightly as though she were preparing herself for the brunt of the backlash.

"So, I'm not fired then?" Lucy spoke slowly.

"Of course not," said Mia, her expression much more cheerful than Steph's. "Even if he hadn't given her an ultimatum, Julia was never considering letting you go. Although...she is going to need some explanation regarding the weak-ass email you sent her with the reason for your absence."

"Period cramps was juvenile to begin with," Steph said wryly as she shook her head. "And that was before Cal decided to explain a little of the truth to Julia."

"Well, that's me done then." Lucy stood abruptly from the sofa, agitation clouding her face. As she turned to face Steph and Mia, she threw up her hands helplessly. "I quit."

Steph's jaw dropped at Lucy's proclamation. "You can't quit," she spluttered.

Jumping up from the sofa, Mia grabbed Lucy's hand in hers. "Don't be silly, Lucy. Don't quit over some stupid guy. It doesn't matter how much he hurt you or how handsome he is, he's not worth tossing in your job over."

Lucy's face grew hot as a mixture of anger and despair filled her. Tears blurred her vision, but she fought to keep them from dampening her cheeks.

"You don't understand," she told them, her voice sharp with pain. "I can't do it. I can't work alongside him for weeks pretending everything's fine." Glancing away from them, her free hand brushed her betraying tears free.

"It'll be alright," Steph told her as she stood to embrace her. "We'll have your back. You won't have to do anything you don't want to do."

"Are you serious?" Lucy protested incredulously. "You know what Julia's like. I'll be doing whatever Cal tells her he wants me to do."

"Aww, honey." Mia sighed sympathetically as she wrapped her arms around them both to make a big group hug.

At their smothering embrace, Lucy's body started

shaking as she tried to fight back sobs. She knew that crying didn't achieve anything, but she couldn't help herself. It had been a long, traumatizing day, and she was terrified of what would happen when—not if—she saw Cal again. She knew she couldn't protect herself forever, keeping him at arm's length.

For fourteen long years she'd fought the urge to contact him, hoping that one day her feelings for him would subside. And they had—or at least, she'd thought they had. She'd let the anger grow until there'd barely been any spark of love left inside her, only hatred. But then she'd seen him again. He'd just waltzed back into her life looking more incredible, more confident, and more alluring than ever. She just knew she didn't stand a chance against him—or her own treacherous heart.

"So, I don't have a choice." Lucy's pained voice was muffled against Steph's black t-shirt clad shoulder.

"Sorry, Luce, but you're out of options," Steph said as she rubbed Lucy's back comfortingly.

"We won't let you quit," scolded Mia firmly, her head resting against Lucy's.

Steph sighed somberly. "And Callum has made it clear he's not leaving until his work with the firm is complete."

Slowly, Steph released them both from the tight embrace and took a step back. Mia followed suit, but still clung to Lucy's arm as though she was the only thing keeping her from collapsing to the ground in a miserable heap.

"So," Steph began authoritatively, "you're going to put on a resting bitch face and come into work tomorrow as a fierce, feisty workaholic who only cares about getting the job done quick enough to get the client moved on. Do you think you can do that?"

Lucy breathed in a full shaky breath. Deep inside she knew that although doing what Steph asked would put her in terrible danger of being hurt all over again, they were right—she really didn't have much of a choice. Even though she'd threatened it and meant every word when it had been released from her lips, she knew she couldn't just quit and give up on everything she'd spent the last ten years working hard for. Her job was her life, and she didn't want to lose that just because of some man.

He's not just any man, her thoughts reminded her. *He's your Cal.*

"Lucy?" Mia was staring at her concernedly.

Wiping her face, Lucy glanced from Mia to Steph and back again. Their worried expressions were enough to make her silently thank the universe for giving her such true friends.

"I know," she told them, her voice deep with resignation. "I'll do my best to keep the peace until it's over and then I'll demand that he and I go our separate ways. That means I'll get to keep my job, Julia can keep her big client, and things can hopefully and eventually go back to the way they were before he arrived."

"I'm glad to hear you're sounding more optimistic," Mia said affectionately.

Steph released a harsh breath. "Optimistic, yes, but maybe not realistic. It's going to be difficult to escape him once his business with the firm is over. Now that he's back in your life, I doubt he's got any plans to willingly withdraw from it again."

Mia shot a glare at Steph and released her grip on Lucy's arm briefly to backhand Steph's shoulder with an audible slap. "What are you doing? We've only just managed to calm her down and now you're ruining it telling her things like that?"

"Sorry," Steph told her, innocently. "I just can't lie to her and say everything can go back to normal after the fact, especially when I don't believe it."

Sighing in frustration, Mia looked back at Lucy. Her annoyed expression morphing with apprehension. "Maybe you could get a restraining order?" Even her voice sounded hopeless.

Lucy glanced between the two women who had been so strong and encouraging only moments before, but who had now seemed infected with her own trepidation. If they didn't have faith that it would all work out, how could she?

For a second, she felt overwhelmed and despondent again. Then, she forced herself to put things in perspective. It wasn't as though her life was ending. She wouldn't be losing her beloved job. The only thing that was changing was Cal's presence in her life—from nothing to a short term working relationship. Once that was over, Lucy knew what she had to do if she wanted him to leave her alone. She had to confess her love for him.

Although it would've sounded ridiculous to Steph and Mia if she'd told them, it made perfect sense to her. She knew that Cal was in no way a one-woman man and was definitely not one to fall in love. Maddy had told her what he'd gotten up to with women in the past fourteen years and Lucy was sure that falling in love was a huge deal breaker. If she told him the truth—that she'd loved him since junior high—he'd be out of her life in a flash and she could go back to her peaceful—if a little loveless— existence. Everything would be fine.

"Everything will be fine." Lucy repeated out loud, recognizing that it was quickly becoming a mantra.

The two women beside her who had been staring at her with worried expressions shared a glance and then seemed to force supportive smiles.

Steph opened her mouth as if to speak and then the doorbell chimed.

Everyone looked toward the hall.

"Pizza's here," Mia said as she reluctantly released Lucy and left the room.

When her girlfriend had disappeared, Steph stepped closer to Lucy. "So, what's your game plan? I know you've got something up your sleeve, otherwise you wouldn't have given in so quickly."

Lucy offered her a shrug. "I guess I just realized that

my biggest weakness might just be the only thing that can save me."

***

"Can't you tell me anything useful?" Cal's voice was gruff as he paced back and forth in Madison and Robert's spacious dining room.

From where they sat watching Cal at the large mahogany dining table, their nearly empty dinner plates before them, Madison gave Rob a worried glance. He shrugged silently, his expression helpless. Madison frowned and then looked over at Cal, who was still pacing the length of the room in front of them, looking unusually disheveled in his loosened grey tie and creased navy suit.

"So, this is why you interrupted our dinner? Because you want to try to force me, for the zillionth time, to tell you why Lucy's upset?"

At Madison's calculated stare, Cal nodded.

"When I saw her today," Cal began.

"What?" Rob raised a hand to interrupt and his strong, wiry frame went rigid beneath his green woolen sweater and blue jeans. "You saw her today? You saw Lucy?"

Madison's mouth opened wide in shock as she watched Cal nod once more.

"Are you serious?" Madison nearly shrieked, her tone filled with elation. Then she stopped and seemed to consider his admission further. Her happy expression fell rapidly, and she covered her lips with the tips of her fingers timidly. "Oh my God, she's going to be furious with me," she breathed.

Rob quirked a brow. "What are you talking about, Mads?"

Gnawing on her lower lip nervously, Madison turned to face her husband. "She'll think I did this. That after fourteen years, I finally caved. I even threatened it in a text the other day."

Cal narrowed his eyes in frustration. "Can we get back to the topic at hand, please?"

At his interruption, Madison shot him a fierce glare. "What did you do, Cal? How did you find her?"

Annoyed by further inquiry on something he didn't have time for, Cal sighed deeply and took a seat at the table beside Madison. With her furious eyes, quivering lips, and the uncharacteristically floral summer dress making her appear more feminine than usual, Cal thought she looked more fearful than fearless.

"Calm down, Madison. It's fine," he told her reassuringly. "I told Lucy that you never told me where she was. In fact, it was completely coincidental, it was like the fates aligned. The manager of my marketing team insisted that I seek the assistance of Insight Marketing to help reinvigorate my father's Gold Coast property. That's all. I didn't realize Lucy worked there until last night when I checked their website."

"See, everything will be fine," Rob told Madison comfortingly as he slipped an arm around her shoulders. "Lucy knows what happened and that you're not to blame."

"Now that that's sorted," Cal said, rising to his feet, the coiled tension in his powerful, brawny build evident, "can we focus back on my issue? I need to know what I did wrong, why she hates me or—at the very least—what I can say to get her to tell me what happened?"

Madison took a steadying breath in and out as she looked up at Cal, but the flicker of concern in her gaze proved she was still rattled. "You have to talk to her yourself, Cal. I'm not getting in between the two of you any more than I already have."

Cal clenched his hands into tight fists, his shoulders high and tight with stress. "But she won't talk to me. She made that obvious today. How can I get through to her?"

Madison furrowed her brow in thought. "You're still working with her marketing firm, right?"

Nodding, Cal crossed his arms over his broad chest. The movement was enough to dislodge the left-side hem of his crinkled, white business shirt from where it was loosely tucked in his navy slacks, causing it to hang freely.

He knew he looked a right sight, an unkempt, unprofessional mess, but at this moment in time he just didn't give a damn. All Cal could think about was how to fix things with Lucy, how to get her talking to him again so that they might begin their friendship anew. And—if he were lucky enough—that they might enter into a new loving relationship together. Tomorrow he could worry about looking decent for her—for his Lucy—but tonight he needed answers.

"Then use that to your advantage," Madison said, snapping Cal free from his thoughts.

"I've already tried," Cal spat in frustration as he paced away from the table before turning back around. "I told her boss that I would only work with the firm if Lucy was on board, that I wanted her to be my direct liaison with the team."

"Cal," Rob said, his deep voice full of reproach. "Did Lucy agree to that beforehand?"

Cal shrugged in exasperation. "What does that matter?"

Madison gasped, her expression part shock, part dismay. "Cal, you're resorting to blackmail."

Pausing in his stride, Cal frowned at Rob and Madison, giving them a look of disappointment that mirrored their own stares of disproval.

"I would've thought that's what you meant when you said *use that to your advantage*." Cal's tone was snappy as he rolled his eyes and turned back on his heel. "I'm only doing what's necessary to get her to speak to me. I need that much before she'll tell me anything."

Releasing a sigh that sounded similar to that of a mother dealing with a challenging child, Madison slapped her hands on the table gently and stood up out of Rob's supportive embrace.

"I'd only meant," Madison explained, "to use the business you're doing with her firm as a means to be around her more often, to try to warm her up to your being there, and hopefully get her to trust you again."

As Cal spun around to begin pacing back toward them, he came face to face with Madison, her expression stern and her hands resting confidently on her slender hips. He met her narrowed gaze with a frustrated glare of his own and pursed his lips thinly.

"I'm not doing this by half measure, Madison. Now that I've found her, I'm not letting her go without a fight."

Madison quirked an eyebrow as though in challenge. "Fine. I only hope you know what you're doing."

Exasperated, Cal threw his hands in the air, his fingers curled like claws. "She already hates me." His voice boomed deeply, aching with anger. "You won't help me with that. So, what's a little blackmail added to the mix? She can't hate me any more than she already does."

At his pained words, Madison's dominant stance relaxed and her firm expression softened, filling with pity and compassion. She breathed another sigh, sounding helpless and resigned, and then opened her arms to him. Cal stared at her for an instant longer, his gaze still clouded and fierce. Then, finally, he took the necessary step forward and let Madison embrace him. Her lean, lithe arms wrapped around his broad, muscular shoulders with difficulty, but she still managed to fit his large bulk into the tight hug.

"You just have to trust that it will all work out," she told him.

Still struggling with his internal fight, desperate to either compel Madison to tell him the truth or find Lucy and force her into his arms, Cal just couldn't hug Madison back. With tension filling his body and his fists clenched, he couldn't do much more than let her try to hold and reassure him.

If he was honest with himself, he knew it wasn't anger

he felt at this whole situation, at Madison, at Lucy. No, instead it was nerves, fear that was creating this furious exterior. And he didn't know how to combat that. He couldn't bear the thought of losing Lucy again, of missing his chance to win her back and convince her that she was his one and only. If he thought his life wasn't worth living before, what would it be like if she disappeared on him again, if he couldn't get through to her and convince her of his feelings? Just the thought of it made his heart ache as though someone were pulling at it, trying to rip it from his insides.

"Just breathe, Cal." Madison's soothing voice cut through Cal's dark thoughts. "I can try to talk to Lucy and do what I can to get her to open up to you. But you have to stop being so hard on yourself and start believing that this will work. Lucy will let you in again."

At those words, Cal pulled out of the hug far enough to see Madison's face.

"Do you mean that? You'll talk to her?" His voice was painfully hopeful.

As Madison nodded reassuringly at their friend, Rob looked on sympathetically, a small smile pulling at the corners of his mouth.

"From what Mads has told me," Rob said slowly, while Cal's gaze found his, "you two were made for each other. I know you've been estranged for a long time, but maybe there's something that's finally drawn you to each other? You have to believe in it, man, otherwise you'll tear yourself apart."

As his brows furrowed in thought, Cal's gaze drifted and he considered Rob's words carefully. After a minute, his dark expression lightened with a look of realization. When he glanced back at Rob and then to Madison, who still stood before him, her hands holding his strong arms supportively, he was nearly smiling.

"I think I know how to get her to open up to me," Cal told them. "First, I need to open up to her."

CHAPTER FIVE

It had taken nearly an hour of apologizing, then explaining and then promising to get Julia to leave her alone and let her get back to work. Fatigued by the whole interrogation, Lucy had gotten to the point of agreeing to things she hadn't even heard or understood properly to begin with.

Julia had needed constant reassurance of where Lucy's loyalty lay and had wanted to know whether or not she wished to see the destruction of a job she'd loved so dearly for a decade. As well as forcing her to be the direct liaison to Cal during all related business dealings and having her promise to agree to all his demands during the process, Julia expected her to do all she could to pique Cal's interest in Insight Marketing and encourage him to look into future business deals with them.

Just thinking about all the things she'd conceded made Lucy shudder. If Julia got her way, Lucy would never be rid of Cal—ever.

With her forehead resting on the cold, hard surface of her desk and her arms wrapped around her ears to silence all external noise, Lucy tried to get her breathing steady in preparation for the day. Although, for the time being, she felt reasonably safe in her office, it had to be almost nine o'clock, nearly time for Cal to arrive—and she knew what that meant.

After sleeping in the guest room at her place last night, Steph and Mia had all but frog-marched Lucy into the office before eight in the morning. They had demanded that she sort out the situation with Julia first before facing the rest of the day with Cal.

When she'd asked them both why they'd had to escort her, Steph had nearly snorted with laughter and disbelief. Apparently, they'd both been certain that if they hadn't accompanied her in that morning, she would never have made it past the threshold of her front door. Although on the outside Lucy had scoffed at them and their act of kind assistance, internally she knew that they were probably right. Without the happiness her friends had added to her morning routine, laughing while cooking breakfast and then cracking jokes on the tram, temporarily removing all thoughts of fear and despair from her mind, Lucy wasn't sure how she would have even made it through the glass doors of the building.

Dread had gripped her as soon as she'd walked toward the internal elevators, even though she'd known that Cal's appointment wasn't for another hour. She might have convinced herself that she had formulated a decent game plan last night, a way in which to deal with Cal should things become too intimate and toxic, but that hadn't stopped her from worrying anyway. What if she couldn't remain emotionally distant in his presence? What if she let him capture her heart like she had once before and she lost herself to him? What if telling him that she loved him became all too true again and his rejection, instead of freeing her, hurt her much worse and deeper than before? Had Steph and Mia not been there literally to hold her hands and steer her into the elevator, Lucy knew she would have sprinted back home right there and then.

But here I am, she reminded herself as she tried to let the coolness of the varnished, wooden desk calm her.

She'd made it in, had managed to smooth things over with Julia and was now awaiting the most difficult task of her life—keeping Cal happy until his business with them had concluded.

A tapping sound like the light rapping of knuckles against the door frame had Lucy lifting her head reluctantly to see Steph waiting outside her office. Upon seeing the movement, Steph opened the glass door and entered, closing it carefully behind her.

"How are we doing?" Steph's smile was hopeful as she moved to sit in one of the pair of black leather chairs in front of Lucy's desk.

Lucy groaned tiredly. "Alive."

As Lucy straightened in her seat, her gaze fell to Steph's outfit. No longer in the crumpled t-shirt and jeans from the night before, she was dressed very professionally in black slacks and a white business shirt with the sleeves neatly rolled up to her elbows. She had told Lucy as they'd left her in front of Julia's office that morning that she and Mia would be heading home to their flat in East Melbourne to change. Yet, seeing it just seemed to further confirm the coming difficulties of the day.

"I'm glad to hear it." Steph struggled with a smile and then leaned forward in the chair. "'Cause our precious new client is currently on his way up in the lift with Julia and you'll have to start liaising at any moment."

Lucy choked in a breath. "Break it to me mildly, why don't you?"

Steph winced. "I had to do it fast like a sticky bandage and hope for the best."

"Well," Lucy breathed deeply, then placed her hands on the desk to help her stand, "I guess I can't just sit here waiting for the beast of the problem to find me. I'll never survive this if I don't jump into the fight."

"You make it sound like you're about to go to war, Luce."

At Steph's criticism, Lucy scowled.

"It is war," she told her. *War of the heart*, Lucy thought. Then she frowned. "Sorry." She shook her head as though trying to clear her thoughts. "I'm already defensive."

Steph breathed in a harsh, audible breath and stood up. "Boy, am I glad that it's him you're at odds with and not me. I don't think I'd like to be on your bad side."

At that, Lucy found herself smiling. She could do this. She could be tough enough to keep things cold and formal between her and Cal. Sure, it didn't come to her naturally, but she could try—and she'd seen plenty of reality television, enough to help her perfect a bitchy persona if she needed it.

As Lucy rounded the table, she saw Mia appear outside, the hem of her pleated, mauve mini-dress swaying with the swiftness of her movement. With a concerned expression and without knocking, Mia opened the office door.

"Cal's here."

She'd barely gotten the words out and stepped inside before Cal appeared in the doorway.

Looking prepared for business in his slate grey suit, white shirt and green tie, Cal strode confidently into Lucy's office.

"Ladies," he said offering Mia and Steph a charming, white smile. "Would you mind giving Miss Spencer and me a moment alone?"

Even though Mia was clearly besotted by the charisma radiating off him, she still took a minute, as did Steph, to glance over at Lucy for approval.

Lucy's eyes were wide, her neck tense and her insides quivered as she stood, frozen to the spot and staring at Cal. How had she ever thought she could be strong enough to do this? Just the suggestion of being alone in a room with him was enough to set her heart racing and her nerves on edge. Who had she been kidding? She wasn't tough and she definitely couldn't pretend to be cold enough to hide the flame for him which still burned ardently in her heart.

Swallowing, she shook her head slowly at Steph.

Seeing her friend struggling to keep her composure and certainly in no state to be alone with a man who clearly terrified her, Steph offered Cal a firm, but amiable expression.

"I'm sorry, Mr. Hawthorne, but we prefer to have an open working relationship and don't like to keep any of our executive managers out of the loop. Perhaps you would like to wait and talk to us together as a group in the boardroom?"

Cal's charming gaze faltered slightly at Steph's words. He opened his mouth to speak just as Julia, all classy and conservative in a crisp, ivory skirt suit, entered the room behind him.

"Steph. Mia." Julia's voice was sharp and authoritative. "Let's give Lucy and Mr. Hawthorne a moment alone together to get reacquainted before we discuss things further as a team."

When Steph opened her mouth to protest, Julia silenced her with an elegant wave of her hand.

"Come, ladies. I'd like to go over a few things before we proceed with the day."

Refusing to wait for a response, Julia turned in her white high heels and disappeared down the aisle.

Mia shared a look of concern with Steph and then both women glanced at Lucy. Biting her lower lip nervously, Lucy's tight, furrowed brows and wide eyes pleaded with them to stay. Yet, she knew they couldn't, not without receiving Julia's wrath.

Her expression solemn, Steph grabbed Lucy's hand, caressing it reassuringly before releasing her and heading closer to Mia.

After eyeing Cal carefully, Mia offered Lucy a small, supportive smile. "We'll be just down the hall if you need us."

"Yes," Steph concurred, her expression stern as she

watched Cal. "Scream if you need help."

Lucy caught the look of surprise on Cal's face as he quirked a sandy-colored eyebrow at the two women as they exited the room, shutting the door slowly behind them. They remained outside for a little longer, staring in as Cal and Lucy stared back, then finally they headed after Julia.

"That was intense." Cal breathed a sigh and then glanced over at Lucy.

When his dark blue-grey gaze met hers, Lucy forced herself to hold it and then swallowed anxiously. "Yeah, I have…um decent friends now." She had hoped the remark would be cutting, bitchy even, but her voice was so soft and unsteady that the intention behind it was little more than weak.

"You mean, guard dogs." Cal smirked, narrowing his gaze as he stalked slowly toward her.

The predatory movement was enough to send Lucy scurrying back around behind the desk for protection. "So, what do you want?" Her fingers gripped the back of her chair so tightly that her knuckles turned white. "You might want to make it quick. We've got a meeting to attend."

His full lips pulled back in a shark-like grin and he plopped himself into one of the chairs in front of her. "Since that meeting largely depends on my attendance, I don't think we have any need to hurry."

Lucy glared down at him, her irritation at his cockiness beginning to override her trepidation. "I'm pretty sure whatever you need to speak to me about regarding the work you'd like us to do for you can be said at the meeting with everyone else. Wouldn't you agree?"

Cal casually crossed his legs, left ankle on right knee, and lounged back into the leather chair as though he felt quite at home in Lucy's office. "Why are you making this harder than it has to be, Luce? You know exactly why I need to talk to you and you know exactly why I don't want it said in front of the others."

"They already know anyway," she spat back, her hands releasing the death grip on her chair to rest in an aggressive manner on her hips.

He chuckled quietly. "I'd noticed."

"No thanks to you." Lucy was glad her tone had outgrown its mousey meekness and had finally reflected the anger that was beginning to boil inside her. "Did you really have to go and tell my boss about our history?"

Cal shrugged. "I only explained what I had to. We had a falling out, which explained your reaction, but now that I have an opportunity to work alongside you, I want to be able to make amends. That's all."

Lucy narrowed her gaze suspiciously. "And what? You promised to pay double our usual fee or something to smooth it all over?"

His lips quirked in a playful smirk. "Triple."

Her eyes grew wide at his insanity. That was an unholy amount of money, an incredible sum that could've easily bought him a nice two-story house in the suburbs.

"That includes acquiring you as my personal liaison."

Lucy suddenly felt faint and she had never been the type of woman who fainted. "You haven't bought me, Cal. You don't own me just because you paid a fee."

With a confident sigh, he glanced around the immaculate office before his dark gaze settled on hers once more. "Buying your time is good enough—and knowing that you have to be at my beck and call whenever I need you, well that's utterly priceless in the circumstances." His lips pulled back into a smug grin. "And just so you know," he told her as he uncrossed his legs and leant forward. "You just called me *Cal.*"

Lucy had never wanted to scream at someone so much in her life, but she just knew it wouldn't do any good. Besides bringing in the cavalry, she would also infuriate Julia and further endanger her position at the firm.

She couldn't believe she'd let herself slip. Calling him *Callum* would've been bad enough, would have sought to break the platonic working relationship she was trying hard to stick to by calling him only Mr. Hawthorne at best and nothing at all at worst. But, *Cal.*

How could she have been so stupid?

"Mr. Hawthorne." Her snide tone was breathy as she tried to control her severe frustration.

Cal waved a hand to dismiss her correction. "No, I prefer Cal and I'll be telling Julia as much. Everyone else can call me Mr. Hawthorne, Callum—but you, Luce, you'll have to call me Cal."

Lucy glared at him. "You're a real bastard, you know that?"

Cal just smiled up at her contentedly as he relaxed back into the black leather chair. "I've missed you too, Luce."

***

Cal had finally gotten his way. Although Lucy had said no repeatedly, when he had threatened to tell her boss that she wasn't cooperating with his demands, she'd finally caved. While the Insight Marketing team looked over the information he'd brought for them regarding the Gold Coast property, he and Lucy would be discussing the same thing—and a little more—over lunch on the Mornington Peninsula.

Even though the director of the firm had been fine with the arrangement, having already been told of his terms as they rode in the elevator together, the other staff he'd met more formally before leaving had definitely not seemed to approve. He hadn't been surprised to see the look of distrust in the eyes of the two women he'd seen in Lucy's office that morning or, for that fact, a similar look of concern on a number of other employees' faces including a short woman with blonde curls who appeared to scrutinize his expression to the nth degree. Yet, the one that worried him the most was definitely the tall, rangy, dark-haired man whose insanely perfect appearance and whose dangerous glint in the eye were enough to have Cal questioning Lucy's relationship with this man and whether or not he had a reason to be jealous.

Glancing across the inside of the black stretch limousine to the adjacent seat, Cal slowly raked his gaze over Lucy and her luscious body. Though she'd chosen to wear less make-up than she'd donned yesterday, the soft, natural shades and dusty rose covering her full lips only added to her exquisite natural beauty. He preferred her this way or with nothing at all. She was stunningly beautiful in her own right, *his Lucy*, and would look gorgeous in every moment—waking up, after going to the gym or after exercise of another kind in bed together with him.

Cal felt a sly smile spread his lips at the thought as his gaze continued to devour her.

Emulating her furious expression, her slender arms were crossed with fierce indignation, but this only served to push her pert breasts even further together forcing him to imagine what it might be like to place his face in that delicately soft Eden. His dark gaze roamed over her tight indigo, knee-length dress, which clung to her curvy body in all the most alluring places, making his groin ache with lust and his mouth water. Even the matching strappy stilettos that wrapped around her creamy skin, bared to reveal just the slightest peek of sexy, red, nail-polished toes, were enough to make him crave to touch her further.

Upon entry to the limo, Cal had offered her a seat beside him, but she'd refused with a non-verbal huff and sat opposite. Though he would have appreciated the closeness, having her body strapped in beside him, he couldn't deny that from this angle he had a much better view of her—and there was plenty of time in the future for them to get closer. Right now, he was just savoring the fact that he'd found her and that she was finally back in his life.

"Are you going to keep staring at me like that the whole way?" Her sharp growl dragged him free of his mischievous thoughts. "Because it's creeping me out."

Cal had to chuckle at that. He was almost certain it was doing nothing of the sort and if anything, seeing the way a light blush had pinkened her cheeks, she'd obviously been enjoying his gaze as much as he was relishing looking at her.

He shrugged. "I haven't seen you in a long time, Luce. What did you expect me to do?"

She threw up a hand. "Well, not look at me as though you want to eat me for one."

Cal had to laugh at that. He'd known he'd been watching her hungrily, there was no denying it. "Maybe if you'd come sit closer to me"—he rubbed a hand over the bare, black leather of the cushioned seat beside him—"I wouldn't have to stare at you so much."

She quirked a brow as though in accusation and then gave him a curt, sardonic smile. "I'm fine here, thanks. Really."

Cal struggled not to laugh again. He'd really missed their play fights, her stubbornness and his going head-to-head. He'd always enjoyed a good challenge, but this time he knew it was a little different. This time they weren't playing for fun, he was playing for keeps.

"Are we nearly there yet?" Lucy's arms tightened across her chest as she glanced back out the window.

"My, aren't we impatient?" he teased her. "I thought you might prefer the scenic route."

Though she'd scoffed at him in annoyance, she was sure to know what he'd told her was a lie. They'd been travelling on the freeway for just over an hour and were about to turn off toward Red Hill. The Cardinal Winery was booked for lunch at noon, so the scenic route would just have to wait.

Having had his epiphany earlier that morning, Cal had called Jonathan—his P.A.—and asked him to hire out the entire winery for the afternoon, no matter the cost. Securing alone time with Lucy was precious, a least until she had the desire to initiate that alone time with him herself. While he hoped that might happen sooner, he was sure it would probably be later. He had a lot of sucking up, a lot of wooing, a lot of breaking down her towering walls, before she would want to spend time with him naturally. Like a child thrilled about the coming Christmas, Cal could barely breathe thinking about the elation he'd feel when Lucy finally saw him as she once had, craving to be with him as much as he craved to be with her. But this time he wouldn't put their friendship first. No matter what, she would finally be his, just as he had always been hers.

CHAPTER SIX

Of all things, Lucy hadn't expected the exclusive winery's lavish restaurant to be empty. Though she'd never visited before, she had heard from friends, Steph and Mia especially, just how impressive and popular the Cardinal Winery was. There had even been whispers that a three-month waiting list stood for all new bookings, but clearly Cal had proved that wrong. If you had enough money, you could achieve anything.

She'd known that Cal's family was well-to-do back in school, but things hadn't really started to take off for them until Cal was a senior. When Cal was young, his father, Phillip, had owned a few properties, his first being the Calypso on the Gold Coast in Queensland. Being good friends with Cal had meant that she and Maddy had been lucky enough to holiday there numerous times at his dad's request, keeping Cal and his cousin Tobias Sutton company. It was an idyllic property, right on the beach, and she'd created some extraordinary memories there—playing hide and seek in the lobby, stealing ice-cream from the humongous walk-in freezer in the kitchen, and trying to make a vortex in the swimming pool by going around and around the edge. Yet, it wasn't until Cal's father had taken a huge risk by buying a giant skyscraper in Melbourne that he really hit the big time in the property market.

In some ways, Lucy felt she should count herself lucky to have known Cal when he was younger. That Cal had been so down-to-earth, so kind and completely unaffected by his family's wealth. He'd been tenderhearted and generous, a really great guy, a best friend, definitely not the pretentious spoiled brat many children with money turned out to be. That was, until junior year when he'd come back from the summer holidays, having travelled through Europe with his family, and decided that he was going to date all her girlfriends, save for Maddy. That had been bad enough. Yet now, she could see it had all finally caught up with him. He no longer held the same personality of that sweet, modest child she'd once known, but had become instead a conceited, entitled womanizer who clearly thought he could buy everything—and everyone.

That was, everyone except for her or her friendship, no matter how much of his fortune he wasted in trying.

"I thought we might prefer the privacy." Cal gestured toward the expanse of the restaurant with its rustic décor, cathedral ceiling with exposed wooden beams and two full walls of timber framed picture windows.

Although the room appeared to be presented in its usual format, selectively spaced chunky cedar dining tables surrounded by wrought iron chairs with decorative scrolls and plush plum colored cushions, only one table in a small, private conservatory-like nook in the far-right corner appeared to be laid with tableware.

Lucy shot him a look of displeasure. "You mean, you think it will be easier to convince me of the sincerity of your intentions without a lot of strange people around."

With a cunning grin, Cal nodded. "Exactly."

She huffed in annoyance. "Fat chance."

As his warm palm met the small of her back in an effort to lead her farther into the room, Lucy skipped quickly from his grasp as though she'd just been burnt.

Him touching her was definitely a no-no. The more distance she could place between the two of them, even at the dining table, the better. She didn't trust herself in his arms, no matter how slight the physical touch. It had been bad enough yesterday, but at least the shock of seeing him after so many years had fueled her with enough fury to ignore the fiery sensations of his touch on her skin.

Today presented another problem entirely. Alone in an intimate setting, her thoughts constantly drawn back to the depths of those enthralling smoky-blue eyes, that teasing, kissable smile, imagining the feeling of her fingers raking through that soft sandy-colored hair—it was enough to have her panting just at his proximity.

Lucy couldn't believe she could still feel this way after so many years. Why couldn't she just grow up and grow out of this *phase*? It was all he was ever going to be to her. Just a phase, a foolish lustful phase brought on by teenage hormones and nothing more. It was purely mind over matter, that's what she needed to focus on. But she knew—though it might have been easy enough to talk sense into her mind—convincing her body, her heart, her very soul was like wishing for a miracle.

"Can you stop smiling at me like that? You look like the shark who scored the seal." Lucy glowered at Cal as he gestured for her to sit on the chair he'd just withdrawn from the table.

"I guess I am," he told her proudly, helping her to adjust her seat before taking his own. "But this," Cal continued, his index finger swirling in front of his pearly white grin, "comes naturally when I'm happy and since today is probably the best day of my life, I'm feeling pretty damn happy, so it's staying."

Even though she felt that evil organ, her heart, do a little flip-flop in her chest at his admission, Lucy rolled her eyes at him, her expression full of disdain.

Sure, he was happy, she thought to herself, *happy to get his hooks into me again.*

Once they were both seated, a petite waitress with perfectly styled blonde hair hurried over to their table with a bottle of wine and nearly curtsied as she showed Cal the label. Following his nod of approval, she opened the bottle and filled their glasses with the deep burgundy-colored alcohol.

As Lucy inhaled the rich, intoxicating aroma, she watched the waitress eye Cal with keen interest. Though she angled her buxom chest closer to him, hoping to catch his eye, Cal's gaze remained firmly fixed on Lucy. Feeling uncomfortable under his stare, Lucy shifted in her chair. His blue-grey eyes seemed to be filled with the promise of dark desires and the sight of them sent a tingling sensation through her core. But she had to be seeing things. Cal had never had any of those desires for her and never would. He'd made that obvious back at school when he'd dated almost every other girl in their clique besides her.

The blonde, busty waitress appeared to be hovering, waiting for Cal to look at her. When he finally pried his eyes away from Lucy, the waitress grinned triumphantly.

"Is there anything else I can get you, sir?"

Cal shook his head politely. "No, thank you. Just leave the bottle."

Instead of placing the opened bottle of red wine on the table as was customary practice, the waitress handed it carefully to Cal, winked and then scurried off in her black kitten heels.

Lucy frowned at the odd behavior and watched as Cal placed the bottle on the table, a piece of paper separating in his hands as he did so. He glanced at it, frowned, and then crushed it in his palm.

"What is that?" Lucy asked instinctively, unable to hide her astonishment.

Cal shrugged and shook his head. "Nothing really."

When she reached out for it, he handed it over without argument. As she began to unravel the paper, she glanced over at the tasting bar where the waitress had been waiting and watching since leaving them. Catching her gaze, the waitress looked suddenly spooked and hurried away into a back room.

Puzzled, Lucy looked down at the smoothed piece of torn paper in her hands and it all began to make sense.

"A phone number? She slipped you her phone number even though she could see you were dining with another woman?"

After a nonchalant shrug, Cal lifted his glass and took a sip, swishing the wine around in his mouth like an expert before swallowing. "Ah," he breathed, his gaze returning to Lucy's. "Their cabernet sauvignon is my favorite."

Feeling a little miffed at the nerve of the restaurant's waitress and by the completely casual reaction Cal had exhibited to such an improper gesture, Lucy felt her expression become stern. "You're not concerned by this at all, are you?"

An innocent frown pulled at Cal's lips. "Should I be?"

Lucy's brows raised. "Don't you think it's a tad inappropriate?"

Carefully, Cal placed his glass back on the tabletop and watched Lucy closely, his expression quizzical. Then a smirk twitched at the corner of his mouth and he leaned forward, arms resting on the wooden table. "Are you jealous, Luce?"

It was said so quietly with such goading charm that a shiver tickled up Lucy's spine and goosebumps broke out across her arms.

"Don't be ridiculous." Her retort was softer than she'd planned and it was nearly a question, not a statement with bite as she'd hoped.

An eyebrow quirked as if in challenge, but Cal remained silent.

"You're acting as though this happens to you all the time," she told him, forcing criticism into her tone.

Cal smiled knowingly. "It does."

Lucy was too slow to catch her jaw before it dropped. Well, no wonder he believed he was God's gift to women, when he had attractive women everywhere just throwing themselves at him. The proof was in the pudding, so to speak, and Cal's pudding was as delectable as hell—even she was having trouble ignoring the handsome, rock-hard outer layer.

Shaking her head, Lucy tried to focus on the task at hand. This was a work-related lunch, that was all, and whatever Cal wanted to do when random women offered up their contact details—like this little, blonde minx had— that was his personal business and didn't concern her. Even though Lucy felt as though she might growl territorially if the waitress came back, Cal wasn't *hers* and she had no claim to him—no, Lucy definitely didn't want him. Did she?

"Try the wine." Cal's deep, tender voice dripped with charm and broke through Lucy's spiraling thoughts.

Obediently and in an effort to quell her nerves, she took a long sip. The fragrant liquid was warm, spicy, but deliciously smooth. "It's lovely," she agreed, before taking another sip, fighting the desire to scull the whole glass and enjoy the languid embrace of tipsiness.

Cal grinned. "I wasn't sure if you'd like it. I only remember you as a beer and tequila girl from back in the day."

Frozen, glass poised to lips, Lucy felt her cheeks grow hot and hoped the developing blush was the result of the strong wine, not her embarrassment at his comment. Slowly, she lowered the glass to the table and began nibbling at her lower lip.

"Toby's parties, you mean?" Her voice sounded nervous, even to her.

Cal's grin widened and he nodded. "You held the record for the most tequila shots downed in thirty seconds. Nine, if I remember correctly."

"And a half," she amended meekly. "But that was a

very long time ago. I'd be lucky to get through a third of that now and still survive the hangover the next morning."

He chuckled. "Know the feeling. I haven't had a night like that in years. Toby still has wild parties though, but now they're cocktail parties and the only thing that's wild is the entertainment."

Relaxing slightly, whether from the wine or from reminiscing, Lucy smiled. "That's right, Maddy told me he was some big deal in the Melbourne Theatre Company."

"He's their theatrical producer."

Lucy could hear the pride in Cal's voice. She chuckled as a memory revealed itself—Toby after one too many drinks performing a monologue as Puck from *A Midsummer Night's Dream* and trying to get all of them, some of them drunker than him, to echo. It had been a garbled mess of words from his fascinated, yet highly intoxicated crowd, but that had never dimmed the passion in his eyes.

"Not an actor himself, then?"

Cal laughed. "No, he tried that, but preferred being in control too much. Remember how he used to get us to put on his plays in front of my parents? He even had us create tickets so he could collect them at the door and usher my mom, dad and Mr. Gillies to their seats."

A grin spread itself comfortably across Lucy's lips as the memory washed over her. For two weeks, nearly every summer, all four of them would spend at least a few days during their stay at the Calypso planning, then performing Toby's eccentric productions. They would always take place in the Great Hall, on a makeshift stage before three lonely chairs—one for Cal's dad, one for his mom and one for Mr. Gillies, the hotel manager. It had been just one of the many things she'd loved about their vacations together and the extraordinary, beguiling establishment that was the Calypso.

Lucy nodded. "They were good times, Cal."

He looked suddenly hopeful. "We can still have good

times together, Luce."

Her smile faltered slightly and she began to chide herself mentally for getting caught up in the moment and lost in fond memories.

"I guess it's time to get down to business," she told him, her tone polite, but more formal.

When his eyebrows furrowed ever so slightly from the ache of rejection, Lucy tried to ignore the mirroring stab of pain in her own heart.

No matter what he says, she reminded herself, *he doesn't really care. He's just using you.*

If that was true, then why did he keep looking at her like that—as though he did care about her, as though he'd missed her, as though he loved her?

*

After ordering, they'd eaten not quite in silence, but close to it. Small chatter was all Lucy seemed to be able to offer him now. Although Cal kept trying, asking numerous questions, some sociable, some personal, he'd received only the briefest of responses in reply. Desiring to know what his Lucy had been up to in her past fourteen years without him, he'd persevered gallantly, not wanting to give in to the topic of business until he truly had to. Yet, the more he persisted, the more he began to wonder if the topic of business might be, in fact, just what was needed to help her relax and start to let him in.

Cal had been surprised at how quickly the protective walls around Lucy's psyche had started to crumble when they'd reminisced about the past, especially their time spent together playing in the hallowed halls of his beloved Gold Coast property. The adventures they had back then had been enjoyed thoroughly by all four of them and Cal was in no doubt that Lucy's memories of their time together were bound to be as wonderful as his own.

Having given him the briefest of answers to his question about what she got up to on the weekends, with "work" and "exercise" being the predominant words used to reply, Lucy was back to gazing through the tall, clear window beside their table and out into the flower garden, the vineyard and the lush, rolling hills beyond.

Realizing he was left with only one option, Cal sighed. "So, I gather from your indifference throughout lunch that you are keen to know more about why I require the assistance of Insight Marketing?"

Lucy's gaze jumped back to his at the sound of his more formal tone. Although her smile was pleasant, Cal thought he could see a slight suspiciousness to her expression.

"If you think we've got enough of the niceties out of the way, then yes, I'd love to talk business." Her smile was almost mocking now and her tone a little too triumphant for his liking.

"I need your help to save something we both love."

Her eyebrows furrowed at his words and she was no longer looking as confident as she had only seconds ago. Cal felt himself smirk at her surprise.

"Something we both love?" Lucy repeated the phrase back to him as though hoping it would clarify itself. She frowned, then shook her head. "I don't know what you mean."

Cal smiled, feeling something of his own victory in finally being able to have the upper hand again. "The Calypso," he told her.

Her expression cleared in recognition and then quickly filled with concern. "What about the Calypso?"

"It's to be put on the market in May." Cal felt a stab of pain in his chest as he said the words. Though they were still true, he wanted more than anything to deny their truth. He couldn't lose his father's beloved property, his second home. Just thinking about it caused more pain to build and the tightness in his chest to grow.

"What?"

He was glad to hear the outrage in Lucy's voice, the same tone he'd used with Jack when he'd been told the news. It was reassuring to know that at least on this topic, they both cared for a similar outcome.

"You can't sell it! It's part of our history," she continued, becoming further indignant.

"That's why I need your help and the help of the Insight team. The whole place needs a revamp, both physically and in the sales and marketing sector. I need to increase guest numbers and make a substantial profit by the end of April or relinquish the deed to the board and have them put the property up for sale."

Wide-eyed, Lucy rested her elbows on the table and laced her fingers together as she nibbled at her lower lip. "A month? We've only got a month from tomorrow?"

Cal offered her a small shrug, his hands clasped together on the tabletop in front of him only inches from where hers lay. "A month and a bit."

She narrowed her eyes at him, her gaze hot with annoyance. "It's the first of April tomorrow."

He dismissed her comment with a shake of his head. "Fine. A month then."

As a deep sigh escaped her lips, Lucy removed her hands from where they'd rested near his and covered her face. When she dropped them down to the table again, they were closer to Cal's.

"I can't believe you're asking me to do this. Us," she corrected herself. "Insight Marketing, I mean. A month isn't long enough to complete a project like this. A month might be the planning stage."

"The physical improvements need to be completed within three weeks," Cal explained. "Less if possible. I want all contractors off the premises by the twenty-first, so that we can put further emphasis on sales and start getting more guests in."

Clearly overwhelmed, Lucy shook her head and then drank the rest of her wine. "I don't know if we can do this, Cal."

He smiled warmly when she said his name. "Julia's

already made her promises and I've signed the contract. Your team's looking over the property's specifications as we speak. I know you can do it. My marketing guys said you were the best freelance firm around and I'm sure of it. Julia was confident I could sign off on all contractors by Friday, to begin work the following Monday."

Lucy shook her head again, disbelief clouding her face. "This is insane."

Finally, Cal took advantage of the opportunity that had been presented to him. Reaching out, he wrapped his big, warm hands around hers, making her fingers look elegant and delicate beneath his. He held her turquoise blue gaze and offered her a tender, honest smile. "Any team that has my Lucy at the forefront is bound to be able to achieve miracles."

For a brief instant, he saw Lucy's smile reach her eyes, a blush pinken her cheeks, then her expression dimmed and her face hardened. She pulled her hands free from his and Cal let her, careful not to show the extent of the disappointment he felt at her rejection.

No, it wasn't a stab to the heart that he felt, he reminded himself, but the spur of the hunt, a proactive pain to prompt him to fight harder.

Composed once more, Lucy casually glanced out the window before carefully returning her gaze to his. "If a month is all we have to achieve miracles, as you say, then you can be sure that all of us at Insight Marketing will do everything in our power to make your endeavor a successful one."

Cal felt himself sigh at the formality of her tone and the coldness in her polite grin. As Lucy began to turn her attention once again to the picturesque surroundings beyond the winery's restaurant, Cal recognized another opportunity.

"Let's take a walk," he told her. He'd made it a statement, almost a demand, so that there was no way she could squirm out of it.

Worriedly, she opened her mouth to answer, then seemed to think better of it. She frowned. "Where?"

Trying to contain his victory, Cal smiled mildly and motioned out the window to the striking scenery beyond. "You seem to be captivated by the place, so let's take a better look around."

Lucy swallowed. "Are you sure? Shouldn't we be getting back to the office? Don't you want to see how the others are progressing?"

Her tone was abuzz with nerves and Cal couldn't help but take some satisfaction in unsettling her. He hoped that maybe this time, maybe during their walk through the wilderness she would finally start to let him in. He wanted her to be comfortable with him again, have the ease of the close friendship they had once shared, have something solid to build on before he confessed his love for her, before he told her that he couldn't live without her and that he wanted to share the rest of his life with her.

"I'm confident they can handle things without us for a while longer," he said. Then he stood and offered her his hand. "Shall we?"

CHAPTER SEVEN

It seemed silly to her now, to have brought the wine with them on their walk, but she'd needed something, some kind of crutch to get through their time alone together—and this time they had been alone for real. There hadn't been any flirty waitresses or helpful bystanders, or limo drivers or work colleagues just down the hall. No, they were out wandering the countryside beyond the Cardinal Winery all by themselves—alone.

Lucy stumbled slightly in the overgrown grass that filled the vineyard row between two lines of flourishing vines full of clusters of plump purple grapes. Glancing down at the oversized, black rubber boots on her feet, she silently cursed the galoshes the vineyard staff had provided for them to complete their trek. Besides being awkward to walk in, they were also a constant reminder of her hindered escape, since there was no possible way she could run in them should things with Cal take an intimate turn.

"Here, let me," Cal said as he removed the dark glass bottle from her grasp. "I think this may be putting you off balance."

Lucy had wanted to refuse him, wanted to fight for her alcoholic crutch, but she knew it'd be useless and that he'd only get his way, anyway. It was obvious he was used to having things just so, used to getting that which he wanted. Besides, there were other more important things to fight Cal on—like getting him used to the fact that rekindling their friendship was no longer on offer.

While she may have appeared far too fond of the bottle, a stumbling dipsomaniac of sorts, it wasn't as though she'd actually gulped the wine or chugged straight from the cold lip at the tip of the neck. Though she may have taken one sneaky sip as they'd strolled outside, she'd barely thought about drinking it during their trudge through the vineyard. If anything, the bottle had been brought along to keep her hands busy and to remove them from the danger of accidentally falling into his. It had seemed a sort of romantic temptation, walking through the magnificent botanical scenery, side by side as the afternoon waned and the sky warmed. She just hadn't trusted herself not to fall into that trap and hadn't wanted to risk him falling into it either. But now he had the bottle and her hands were empty. Now all she was left with was her own self-control and she knew that didn't bode well at all.

Wringing her hands together as they walked, Lucy tried to force herself to relax. Boy, did she wish she had pockets. Whose idea had it been to wear a slinky, indigo dress anyway?

"I wasn't sure you'd hand it over so easily." Cal's deep, silky tones woke Lucy from her fretful thoughts.

"What?" Her voice came out in a pathetic peep as she tried to get her mind in order.

Cal waggled the wine around in front of him and grinned teasingly.

"Oh. Yes. No."

Quirking an eyebrow at the vagueness of her answer, Cal searched Lucy's face. "What made you bring it along?"

Lucy swallowed nervously and then tried to shrug nonchalantly. "It's good wine."

Accepting her answer, Cal nodded and then took a sip

for himself. As he lowered the bottle again, he let out a sigh of pleasure. "That it is."

Lucy forced herself to smile and then to stop wringing her hands. What did she really have to fear? Their conversation had been innocent since they'd left the restaurant. They'd discussed the weather, the winery, Cal had spoken about his work and told her more about his plans for the Calypso. He hadn't continued to reminisce with her as he had earlier and, though she feared it, there seemed to be no danger of the conversation or the situation becoming intimate.

With a deep, steadying breath, she relaxed herself slightly and tried to enjoy the stunning location. "It's truly beautiful, isn't it?" Although she spoke the words aloud, they had almost escaped her of their own accord, as though such a strong internal admiration had to be released to the world.

"I'm glad you think so," Cal agreed. "Because I've made sure we'll have tonight and tomorrow to enjoy it."

His words hit Lucy like a hammer to the back of the head. She froze on the spot and her jaw dropped.

"Pardon?" She knew her tone was abrupt, rude even, but she couldn't help it.

What the hell had he just said? Tonight and tomorrow? Together?

She was suddenly feeling very cornered by his announcement and her disobedient mind fell blank in its effort to offer escape routes.

Coming around to stand in front of her, Cal offered her a reassuring smile. "I've arranged for us to stay the night," he continued slowly, but with recognizable charisma. "In separate rooms, of course. I've checked it with Julia. She agreed that it would be beneficial for us to spend some more time together—getting on the same page."

Lucy's gaze narrowed on his, suspicion clouding her vision. "For the project?"

Cal nodded. "For the project."

Frowning, Lucy took a step away from him, toward the main house of the winery estate. "Maybe I should give Julia a call? To double check."

With a pleasant grin, Cal shook his head. "No need. I phoned her before to get confirmation."

"That was the call you had to make after lunch?"

He nodded again.

Lucy couldn't have felt more trapped. One of the few things getting her through this whole experience was the knowledge that she would be going home soon—alone—and that she would be able to process the events of the day—by herself—in order to get things back in proper perspective and remind herself that these strong feelings she had for Cal, made worse when she was around him, were unfulfilling at best and ridiculous at worst. She desperately needed that space away from him and, if she didn't get it, she feared wanting to hold his hand during a romantic stroll would be the least of her problems.

In a gesture that seemed both temptingly sweet, yet quite outdated, Cal offered Lucy his arm.

"It must be getting on. Shall we head back? I can show you to your room and we can get settled before dinner?"

As Lucy opened her mouth to answer, to remind him that they'd only just eaten lunch, the dusty pinks of the sky and the sight of the falling sun stopped her. They must have finished lunch hours ago and while she did note the gentle rumblings of a building hunger, it completely shocked her to think that they'd spent so much time together, roaming the vineyard, talking. Although Cal may have behaved himself, keeping to safe, surface topics, he'd still managed to bond with her through all the stress and anxiousness, creating a space in which time moved quicker, in which she must—though she hated to admit it—have actually enjoyed his company.

Glancing down at the galoshes on her feet, Lucy tried to decide how best to proceed. Did she continue to try to fight Cal on his inconvenient arrangement? Did she ignore him and call Julia anyway or did she just bite her tongue and take his arm? It was in this instant of turmoil that she realized a bigger problem.

Looking up at him, Lucy felt her expression become more helpless than she would've liked. "I can't stay overnight. I haven't brought anything with me."

Cal's grin widened and without further hesitation, he slipped his arm through hers.

The sensation rocked her and stole away her already shallow breath. His hard, muscular arm was pressed so close to her, so tantalizingly close to her side and to the plump, fabric-covered flesh of her breast. From the thrumming nucleus of his touch, sparks of electricity vibrated and tingled to the furthest reaches of her body. She shivered.

"No need to worry, Luce," he told her as his warm, rough palm covered the smooth, supple skin of her hand. "It's all been sorted."

With her mind distracted by the deliciousness of his proximity, Lucy was powerless to stop him as Cal turned her and began guiding her back to the main building of the Cardinal Winery estate.

***

Lucy wondered how Cal had managed to keep his plans a secret for so long. He hadn't been lying when he'd said that he'd had the situation "sorted".

As she washed her hands at the porcelain sink in the modern bathroom attached to her private room, Lucy glanced over at the neat arrangement of toiletries on the black marble countertop beside her. He'd included everything she could have wanted. Shampoo, face wash, moisturizer, toothbrush, razor, hair brush, hair straightener, etcetera, the array of cosmetic products continued. Yet, this display had surprised her just slightly less than that which she'd been confronted with once she'd first opened the door to her room.

While simply styled with minimal necessities—a bed, desk, chair, and closet—the room was cleanly contemporary, but warmed with lush, wooden antiques and a large, bright picture window framed with crimson curtains. In the center of the queen-size bed, atop the ebony and gold bedsheets, sat a robust gift basket of wine, chocolates, and other goodies, surrounded by neat little bundles of clothes. Tied with gold ribbon in tidy parcels of like items, each pile presented something different—a choice in bras, panties, and pajamas.

Then, when she'd turned her attention to the closet and opened the elegantly carved mahogany doors, Lucy had tried not to gasp. An assortment of stunning dresses, sleek pant suits and casual wear filled the space, while below shoes of various styles—heels, flats, sandals—were placed perfectly paired on the closet's floor. It was an extravagant spectacle, an amount of special spoiling just for her the like of which she'd never experienced before in her lifetime and which had her wondering whether she ever would again.

It had been a little over an hour since Cal had left Lucy to the privacy of her own room to get ready, and she was sure he'd be due to collect her for dinner very shortly.

After turning off the faucet, Lucy dried her hands and then looked over her reflection in the huge fluorescently lit bathroom mirror.

Out of the enormous selection of outfits she had to choose from, Lucy had opted for yet another slinky dress. Even though a pant suit had seemed a safer option, putting a fabric barrier between her and making a carnal mistake, she hadn't thought it would quite suit the occasion of a fancy dinner at a prominent restaurant.

Lucy smoothed the shiny black silk of her floor-length dress, ensuring the thigh-length slit up the side remained modestly closed and then adjusted the gold metal straps over her shoulders. The high neckline sat at her collarbone and the snug material clung to her hips, cinching at her waist. She admired the way the dress seemed to make her appear much curvier than she actually was. As someone who always felt average in appearance, it was satisfying when something actually made her feel pretty—beautiful even—but that seemed to be a rare occurrence.

Turning to glance over her shoulder to get a better look at the open back which revealed the even pale of her bare skin and dipped below her waistline, Lucy reminded herself that this sexy attribute of the dress was why she'd decided not to wear a bra. Of course, it was more than likely that she'd chosen not to wear one because of the sensual sensation of the material against her naked flesh. Or because of the memory of Cal's body so close to hers, the tingling pleasure of his touch making her desire more, but she'd blame those reasons on her subconscious and not let her conscious self take any responsibility for the decision.

Moving back to face the mirror, Lucy's fingertips went to her lightly made-up face. She'd neatened her brown eyeshadow and black mascara with the cosmetics from her own handbag, but used the light coral blush and dark pink lipstick that had been provided for her by Cal. A few wisps of her dark hair curled softly around her face adding further to the feminine sexuality exuding from the dress, while the rest had been piled and pinned loosely atop her head.

While her host had also included a choice of exquisite jewelry had she desire to change, Lucy had kept her plain gold hoop earrings, certain she wouldn't feel comfortable wearing something that was sure to have cost above her daily wage or more. Glancing down at the matching black and gold stilettos that completed her outfit, Lucy hoped that this time she wouldn't be swapping her shoes for another pair of galoshes.

As she left the attached bathroom and returned to the

spaciousness of her room, she heard a soft knocking sound. Though she looked at the door which led outside, she was almost certain that the noise she'd heard hadn't come from that direction, but from the wall to the right of her, near a bright cream painted door she hadn't yet investigated. She had assumed it to be a built-in closet and, as she had already been more than pleased with the contents of the first mahogany one, she hadn't thought to see what was inside.

"Cal?" She said his name as she glanced between the two options.

Is he behind door number one or door number two, she wondered. *And if so, where exactly did door number two lead?*

"Luce?" His voice sounded wary. "I'm at the adjoining door. I've unlocked my side, but you've got to unlock yours."

The adjoining door?

Her gaze snapped to the right, to the bright cream color of door number two.

Yes, she'd heard that correctly. Cal had organized adjoining rooms. She would have been furious had the knowledge of it not sparked some deep enticement to tug at her libido.

She considered telling him to head around to the front, not wanting to unlock the door between the rooms and add further temptation to what her slinky black dress was already offering—but she didn't.

Without a word, she walked over to the door and placed her hand on the cold brass handle.

"Lucy?" His tone was cautious again.

With a flick of her thumb, she turned the lock and then twisted the handle. Her breath caught in her throat as she pulled the door toward her, slowly revealing the tall, broad handsome figure behind it.

Cal was elegantly dressed, matching her quite perfectly in his jet-black suit, white fitted shirt and gold and silver tie.

Lucy tried to breathe, she knew she needed air, but the scrumptious sight of him kept each breath too shallow. She felt like some kind of animal, like a creature that had been caged too long without food and now found itself face to face with an extraordinary meal. The feminist in her was irked at the comparison, at the thought of Cal as a potential piece of meat, but she knew the reality was much worse than that. She had hungered for him nearly all her life and now here he was, presented to her in such a perfect situation—adjoining rooms, for heaven's sake—that her once tight control over her lustful desires was ever weakening.

"Hi, there." It was more of a purr from his lips than a greeting.

Lucy's gaze rose to his and she saw a hunger there that seemed to mirror her own.

"Adjoining rooms, Cal?" She had hoped it would be a playful accusation, instead it came out with a betraying hopeful lilt.

His sexy smirk in return seemed to promise things that Lucy was sure her sex-starved mind was falsely interpreting. Those sparkling teeth weren't promising to nip at her flesh in all the right, intimate places. Those luscious lips weren't vowing to devour hers and yet, that's exactly what her mind was imagining.

Lucy forced herself to breathe. "Are we going through your room to dinner?" This time it came out with just the right amount of mockery.

Cal chuckled. "You've caught me. Dinner will be held in my room."

Once again, Lucy was left with visions of the hunger they could sate with their mouths locked to one other, then on supple skin and taut flesh as their lips roamed each other's naked bodies.

Another deep, shaky breath failed to calm her.

He was kidding, she told herself, *he had to be kidding*.

Cal's smile grew wicked as he gestured for her to walk

through and into the danger of his room.

Obediently, Lucy did as instructed, and saw that the space inside was arranged similarly to her own. The only difference that was obvious was that his room looked to be at the edge of the block of elevated units and appeared to have a private balcony at the external end. Or that was what the candlelit table on the porch outside through the open exterior door seemed to suggest.

Lucy paused in step at the sudden realization. They *really were* having dinner in his room or, at least, in sight of it. The slight nervousness that had buzzed through her as she slipped over the threshold turned up a notch and she was left wondering how she would feel about being so close to Cal and to an available bed throughout the entirety of dinner. The mere thought had her mentally chiding herself for not deciding to wear pants. Pants were always safe; a dress was slut city.

"You are unbelievably gorgeous, Luce."

The words were whispered so close to her that she swore she could feel the warmth of his breath on her neck. As she turned her head to glance up at him, Lucy felt his fingertips brush against the bare skin of her back. The gentle touch was like a jolt to her system as though he'd just administered a defibrillator. Her heart raced while hot lust fired through her veins and pooled in her depths, at the very core of her. Her whole body craved him and she knew, if she wasn't careful, that she could easily jump him right then and there and have her wicked way with him.

A little heady at the thought, Lucy compelled herself to step away from Cal, walking deeper into the room. Free of his grasp, she could finally think a little more clearly. With another gulp of air, she spun around to face him, only to find herself at eye-level with his strong, kissable throat only mere inches away.

Lucy swallowed and pushed her hands behind her back, clasping them tightly over the rise of her derriere. Her fingers itched to touch him, her palms burned in anticipation, but she wouldn't let them have their way. It was simply mind over matter, that was all.

"Lucy," Cal asked slowly, a playful inflection drawing out her name. "Tell me what you'd like?"

Her ragged breath escaped her, and she became certain there wasn't any more air left in the room.

You. In that bed. Naked. Her thoughts betrayed her.

Cal quirked a brow. "Chicken or beef? I think the chicken is a risotto. Or I can have them bring something else?"

Any air left in her lungs whooshed out in a relieved sigh, partly because she'd been mistaken in her understanding of his question and partly because she hadn't managed to embarrass herself. Yet.

"Chicken," she told him and definitely felt the part.

He smiled down at her, his alluring smoky-blue eyes glinting slightly as though admitting they knew more than they should.

Without touching her this time, Cal led her out onto the balcony into the crisp, but comfortable night air. He helped her take a seat and then took his own, opposite her.

The small round table was laid with a burgundy colored tablecloth, white porcelain plateware and silver cutlery. Although the tabletop was bare of flowers, the fragrant jasmine blossoms that bloomed along the wooden balustrade of the balcony seemed to add just enough of a romantic atmosphere without seeming cheesy. As it was, they could've been dining on newspaper wrapped fish and chips on the floor and Lucy still would've felt the romantic pull.

"*Bon appétit.*" Cal motioned for her to remove the stainless-steel dish cover from her plate as he followed suit.

Once lifted, the cover revealed all kinds of scrumptious smells and Lucy suddenly felt another hunger rise, not just in the carnal sense. The generously sized risotto was delicate in appearance with its neatly chopped chicken and mushroom pieces, light sprinkling of spices and tidy green garnish. Her stomach rumbled at the sight of it. Pushing aside her desire for Cal, Lucy decided to focus on sating this new hunger, knowing that it was at least something she had control over.

Maybe dinner would help put things in perspective, return her thoughts of their relationship to the platonic working arrangement it should be? Maybe pigs would fly and she could click her fingers and finally be wearing pants? Lucy thought she seemed to be mulling over a lot of doomed maybes.

CHAPTER EIGHT

Cal was doing everything in his power to stop Lucy from leaving. The intimate dinner he'd organized for them to share had been over for an hour, but still they had continued to talk and laugh, reveling in each other's company.

Although he couldn't be certain, Cal was beginning to believe that he'd broken through those internal walls Lucy had held intact to keep herself at a distance from him. She'd let them reminisce on fond topics from their shared past, she'd openly discussed her life now and even let them talk of their friendship during secondary school. It finally felt as though he was making headway, inching closer to the friendship that he had so sorely missed for nearly half his life and getting ever closer to the loving relationship he wished to build with her.

When Cal had discussed his plans with Julia that morning and then confirmed them later that day, having already arranged for all the necessities Lucy could desire to be brought and displayed within her room, he'd never expected things to move so smoothly. In fact, when he'd made the arrangements for them to stay overnight at the Cardinal Winery, he had completely believed Lucy would fight him on the decision, even going so far as to call a taxi to come and take her home. But she hadn't fought him and she'd accepted all he'd planned without so much as a complaint.

It had Cal wondering whether, somewhere hidden inside her, somewhere Lucy wouldn't let him see, there was a part of her that wanted this as much as he did, a part of her that wanted them to be as close as they once had been, maybe even closer than before. That thought had everything inside him hoping and praying that he would end his plight, that he would convince Lucy of his love for her, and that she would complete him and agree to be his other half for the rest of their lives.

But first he had to get her to stay. He didn't want to seduce her, didn't need them to sleep together. Not right now, anyway. He might have longed to hold her close to him, desired to touch and kiss her in all the intimate places he'd dreamed about, thrust into her, and finally feel what it was like to be at home inside her—but all of that could wait. No, tonight was about rekindling that flame. They needed to stay up all night talking the way they used to, they needed to share everything, immerse each other in their respective lives, become one with each other. Maybe after that, maybe tomorrow, they could see what else developed, but Cal had no desire to rush her. He'd finally found her and he wasn't about to scare her away with his desire for her, with his love for her. He just needed her to stay.

Lucy sighed. It was a deeply satisfied sigh. She smiled across the table at him. "I guess we should call it a night."

Cold fear gripped his heart and Cal felt his contented expression falter. He searched his mind for a good excuse and then his gaze landed on the half empty bottle of cabernet sauvignon on the table. "But, we haven't finished the wine." It sounded corny even to his own ears.

Lucy followed his gaze to the bottle with a lazy smirk. "We did manage to finish the *first* bottle, remember. I'm pretty sure starting the second was a good enough achievement."

When he frowned, she laughed at him, forcing Cal to see the funny side and let out a chuckle of his own.

"Are you suggesting, Miss Spencer, that I'm trying to get you tipsy by asking you to stay for another drink?"

Lucy playfully quirked an eyebrow. "Not at all, Mr. Hawthorne," she explained with a giggle. "I'm merely admitting I'm tipsy enough as it is and don't need another drink."

They shared a laugh together.

"I've got to say, I'm feeling a little woozy myself," Cal agreed, but he was willing to bet that his intoxication had more to do with being near Lucy than from drinking the alcoholic beverage.

"Then it's decided." Lucy sighed again as though in disappointment, then placed her hands on the tabletop and stood out of her chair. "Thanks for a wonderful dinner."

As she rounded the table, Cal was quick, jumping out of his seat to follow. His hand wrapped around hers before he'd even thought the movement through. "Do you have to leave?" His voice almost wavered as he asked.

Lucy stopped where she stood, her free hand slightly stretched out toward the open door of his room as though it might be enough to will her to safety. Cal watched her closely as her gaze fell to his hand on hers. Gently, she squeezed her fingers against his and sent a tingle of electricity through him.

It was bad enough that he'd touched her, especially with his plan going so well, but the remaining constant skin-on-skin contact was both driving him to distraction and forcing him to focus on only one thing in particular— how much he'd like to touch the rest of her, everywhere.

When her tranquil blue eyes rose to his, they seemed dark and distant, as though she were lost in the depth of her own thoughts. A long moment passed, then her gaze dropped, and she was staring at his mouth. He stared at hers, his heartbeat racing.

What was she doing to him? He was losing control. He could feel his restraint slipping, his desire building. He needed to release her, to look away from her, but his fingers wouldn't obey.

Then her tongue slipped out, and she licked her lips in one long delicate stroke—and something inside him just snapped.

Lucy was in his arms and Cal had barely pulled her to him. Their lips locked, her soft mouth opening to him. Her supple body melted along the hard line of his as his powerful arms wrapped around her, securing her against him. She moaned low in her throat as he tasted her, tongue, teeth, lips, he probed into her silky depths wanting to devour all of her.

His fingers found the warmth of the bare skin of her back and couldn't help but slip beneath the black material of her dress to caress the smoothness of her waist. Her skin was delectably warm and smelled like honey and jasmine, while her lips still held the sweet tang of the berry sorbet they'd had for dessert. Lucy's hands were around his neck, her fingers entwined in his hair as she held him close, refusing to let his mouth release hers.

Cal felt his mind swoon at the thrill of it, at the desire radiating out of her—out of him, at the thought that this was finally happening. As though he were a man possessed, his hands freed themselves from the temptation of her bare skin momentarily, then grasped around the lush roundness of her bottom, lifting her against him. Instinctively, Lucy's left leg slipped through the side slit of her dress and wrapped around him. As Cal lifted her higher, the soft warmth of her sensual center found the stiffness of him and she let out a moan. Her hand shot down to the right side of her dress, hoisted up the black silk material and in an instant, her silky right leg was locked behind him as well.

Then, he was walking, awkwardly, slowly, almost blind,

unable to control himself, heading inside and searching for somewhere suitable, for the bed. Lucy's soft lips were stealing every ounce of sense from his thoughts. Though he'd been so sure it had been his hunger that had drawn them together, her own matched his perfectly, smothering him, devouring him with every brush of her lips and dance of her nimble tongue.

As she shifted against him, her hot core stroking against the hard, ready length of his erection, Cal's focus turned primal. Her lips left his, her face burrowing into the crook of his neck, tasting the sensitive skin there with a lick and a gentle nibble. Just before his eyes rolled back into his head at the intoxicating sensation, he'd seen his destination.

Cal stumbled forward those last few feet until his knee hit the spongy mattress of the bed, then he climbed up, lowering Lucy there, finally forcing himself to release her to the softness below. Lucy fought to keep his lips to hers as Cal leaned back, struggling to remove his jacket, but then she found better use for her time away from him and began undoing his tie. She had his shirt open and his belt unclasped when he finally kissed her again.

"What are you doing to me?" It was more of a breathy groan than a question as Cal lowered his body to hers.

His groin fit snugly, perfectly, in the burning, wet valley between her legs, making her moan in reply. Her long, limber legs were still wrapped around him, holding him against her, pressing him harder into her. The feeling of her, moist, open and ready for him was driving him insane. He wanted to strip her naked, to strip himself naked, to be lost inside her, thrusting into her, building them both to an unimaginable climax. He wanted to roam her body, lave every inch of it with his tongue, press his lips to those pert nipples, devour that deep, intimate heat between her thighs. His hunger for her was like a wild beast, dangerous, ravenous, and out of control.

Though some small remaining flicker of sense deep

within Cal knew that they might both regret giving in to the moment, it wasn't enough to stop him. As Lucy writhed beneath him, her hands torn between unbuttoning his pants and clenching around the firmness of his buttocks, Cal's last lingering shred of intelligence left him and he was lost to the beast within.

His desperate fingers pulled at the gold straps of her dress, dragging them down from her shoulders to free the generous mounds of her impeccable breasts. Her rosy nipples were pricked firm to attention as his voracious mouth drew them in with a gentle bite, lavishing each one with care, one after the other, unable to choose a favorite. Lucy purred in pleasure, her back arching, thrusting herself toward him as her fingers tangled in his hair.

When she moaned again, her eyes closed, focusing on the sensation, Cal could've sworn she'd said his name, that—in that gasp of sound—she had begged him to continue with a single word.

Cal.

It was enough to make him swell larger, sending a painful ache through him, making him desperate to seek that final release. He pulled the material of her dress lower, his tongue licking a moist trail between her breasts down to her bellybutton. There, he nibbled at the supple flesh, the peaches and cream of that delectable skin. He dipped his head lower, wishing the silky fabric would just disappear. He wanted to taste her, wanted to kiss his lips to that creamy core, to stroke that sensitive flesh with his tongue, with his fingers until she came. He needed to taste her, to know what she was like when she was hot, ready, and wanting him, needing him.

"Cal." She moaned again and this time his name was audible.

It vibrated through him, his name on her lips, her desire, his need. It was building, unrelenting and he was running out of time.

He tore the fabric, the material of her lovely, black silk

dress ripped in his strong hands. Cal groaned hungrily, animalistically, as the ebony lace of her panties revealed themselves. He bent his head lower, his mouth so close to its desired destination, while Lucy sighed and writhed in anticipation.

Suddenly, a loud buzz of vibration turned him rigid—and then the familiar chime of an incoming call began.

Cal swore angrily as he glanced up from his haven between Lucy's legs to see his mobile phone dancing around on the bedside table.

Eyes wide, Lucy propped herself up on her elbows and began covering herself with the torn, black material that was once her dress.

Seeing her expression, Cal swore again.

Lucy's cheeks were flushed and her breathing was ragged, but not because of the exceptional techniques of his sexual prowess. No—it was the terrified look on her face, the churning mixture of embarrassment and fear filling her wide, blue eyes that had caused this reaction. She stared at him as though she couldn't understand how they'd gotten there, as though she was trapped—as though she wanted to run.

"It's okay," he told her, his tone low and calm the way you might speak to a frightened creature. "I can let it go to voicemail."

Although he still ached with desire himself, needing to touch her, to taste her intimately, Cal rose slightly and moved over her, his face inches from hers.

Lucy stared at him, her large eyes quivering, glistening as though holding back tears while her teeth gnawed at her lower lip.

"It's okay," Cal repeated reassuringly as the ring and the vibration of the interrupting call finally ceased. Then he bent his head and placed a gentle kiss to Lucy's swollen lips.

She responded, her mouth welcoming his, but then she broke out of the kiss and turned her head away.

Cal's eyes blinked open at the movement just in time to see a single glittering tear curl its way over her cheekbone before she brushed it away.

"Lucy?" It was all he could say as his own overwhelming fear speared into his heart.

What had he done? He'd let things go too far, let everything get out of control. What did she think of him? Had he just confirmed the womanizing nature she believed him to have? Did she think she was just another one of his conquests? How could he have been so weak, such an idiot? Had he ruined everything?

Cal's stomach ached with heavy dread as he dropped to the mattress beside Lucy and tried to get her to look at him. She dropped her head to her chest and breathed in a deep, trembling breath.

"I can't do this." Her usually sweet voice was strained as though her throat hurt. "I'm sorry. I don't know why…." Lucy's voice trailed off. Another deep breath had her choking back a sob. "Oh God, I'm so stupid."

Cal's heart ached at her words. He'd been the one who'd been stupid, not her. He placed a comforting arm around her shoulders and she let him pull her against him. She was fighting so hard not to cry, but her body still shook as though seeking another more suitable way to release her despair.

It absolutely destroyed him to see her this way, and it was all his fault. He should never have pressed her to stay. His desire for her had gotten the best of him and the whole thing had moved too quickly. And now, what would he do? What *could* he do? Could it be possible that she hated him even more than before?

As he held her closer, he thought that unlikely. She had been with him, after all, lost in the lust that had conquered them both. She'd kissed him with the same passion, touched him with the same desire, held onto him, wanting him with the same fire that he felt burning inside him. Their need had been mutual, he was sure of that—but then why was she so scared? And what was she afraid of?

Suddenly, she pushed away from him. "I have to go." Her words were firm, direct, decisive.

Cal didn't think he could convince Lucy to stay this time. He longed to comfort her, to have her confide in him, explain what terrified her, but she wasn't yet in a state to talk things through.

With a shaky breath, Lucy moved even farther away from Cal on the bed until his arm fell free of her shoulders. Immediately, her rejection ate away at him and it pained him deeply, agonizingly, not to be touching her, consoling her. Although Cal hadn't realized it at the time, her touch had been as comforting to him as he hoped his had been to her. It was all he could do not to reach out and try to touch her again.

As Cal looked over Lucy's nearly nude body, that gorgeous figure, those slender limbs, he searched for something—anything—to say to fix the situation, to make things better, to go back a step to when they were getting along so perfectly just moments ago.

"Let me get you a robe." The blunt, emotionless words were out of his mouth before he had a chance to think them through, think about phrasing them and before he even made a move to get off the bed.

Lucy's gaze shot to his and she frowned at him. There was hurt in her eyes, hurt he didn't really understand. She stared into him, into his being, searching, her eyes narrowed, brows furrowed as if seeking an answer.

Cal had known he hadn't said it right. He'd only thought to be a gentleman, to make her feel more comfortable instead of clutching her ripped dress to her bare chest. He'd thought it might help him too—help him stay focused on repairing the mess he'd made instead of focusing on how much he wanted her naked body beneath him. He'd known the words had left his lips distractedly, coldly even, but they'd been more for him, more of an instruction to tell him to stop acting like a horny bastard feeling sorry for himself and start doing something to make the woman of his dreams feel better.

His mouth fell open. Cal wanted to tell her what he'd meant, wanted to apologize, but the fear of saying something else equally stupid or even more unfeeling had the words catching in his throat.

When Cal frowned at her helplessly, Lucy's face contorted in pain and he thought he could see fresh tears welling in her beautiful eyes.

"Oh—my God," she said, her voice bursting out in sobs. Lucy's hand covered her mouth as though in shock before it fell loosely into her lap again. "I should have known. This isn't—I'm not impor—you don't—" Her voice broke away again. A split second passed and she got abruptly to her feet. "It's fine," she said as she held the ebony material over her chest.

"Luce—" Cal began, his heart aching to correct her as he stood and moved toward her around the bed.

Lucy held up a hand to stop him, refusing to meet his eyes. "It's fine," she said again, her tone harsh, nearly cynical in its depth. "We're fine. It will be business as usual tomorrow, but right now—I have to go."

Cal's heart felt like it was about to explode in his chest and his stomach was heavy with mounting anguish. He didn't know how to mend things, didn't know what to say to convince her that she was wrong. He wanted to tell her he loved her, that he'd loved her his whole life, but he knew that was certain to scare her away faster than the other mistakes he'd already made.

"Do you need anything? I can arrange it to be brought to your room?" His voice was breathy this time, but kind, empathetic.

Cal wanted to beg her to let him stay near her, to stay in his bed while he slept on the floor. He just wanted to be close to her. Fear gripped him deeper at the thought of her leaving him, of him having lost her again forever. He didn't want to let her out of his sight in case she ran from him again. Yet, he knew that wouldn't be possible. She'd made up her mind and no amount of pleading from him would convince her otherwise. He should be grateful that she would be sleeping as close as in the next room. That should have meant something, but it wasn't enough.

"Are you sure you—" *Don't want to stay here*, was what he'd wanted to ask before she cut him off again.

"I can't stay here."

It took Cal an instant to realize she hadn't read his mind and that what she was actually saying was that she couldn't stay *here*—the Cardinal Winery's estate.

"I need to go home. I can't stay here tonight."

Cal felt his mouth open in protest, but still the words didn't come. Shock had frozen his whole body. It was as though everything he'd feared had finally come true. She was leaving him, running away from him again and he didn't know if this would be the last time her saw her for another fourteen years—or more.

His heart exploded or at least it felt like it. He was suddenly breathless, numb, unbelieving. Then his whole body began to ache with such ferocity that he nearly stumbled when he finally found the strength to step toward her.

"I don't want an argument," she told him fiercely, shutting him down again as she walked to the open connecting door. "I just need you to do this for me. I need to go home."

Screw it! He wanted an argument if it would mean that he could win, that she would stay with him. Angry now, not at Lucy, but at his own stupidity, at the situation, Cal felt his eyebrows furrow. His lips parted and he was about to ask her to tell him a good reason why he should let her go, when she glanced up and finally met his gaze.

There was so much pain there, so much anger, so much fear. Cal couldn't comprehend how she could possibly feel that way. Her turquoise eyes were dark with sorrow, hard with a desperate control as they gazed into his and then, all of a sudden, her reasons began to become a little clearer.

Could it be that she loved him? That she actually loved him back? Was that it? Was that the reason she was so terrified?

Lucy had been so desperate to keep things under her control, to focus on work, to keep their relationship platonic, to not reminisce about the past. She'd hidden herself away from him for nearly a decade and a half for God's sake, could it be that she did that because of her love, because of her fear that he didn't love her back?

"I'm going to call a taxi." Her lovely voice, firm though it was, cut through his wandering thoughts.

"No, you're not." He was no longer at a loss for words, no longer shocked, no longer in pain. His Lucy loved him. He could see it now, in her eyes, in the fear, in her escape. She wasn't just trying to protect herself from him, she was trying to protect herself from her own feelings.

Cal finally knew how to make things better, although he couldn't do much tonight. He had to give Lucy the space she needed to calm and clear her head, but he'd also make sure that there was no permanent escape route. Running away from him would not solve her problems, even if she didn't realize it.

"I'll have my chauffeur drive you back. I'll call him. He's staying in a room at the main house. I'm sure he'll be ready in less than half an hour."

Lucy moved to protest, but it was Cal's turn to cut her off.

"He can take you straight home and return for me in the morning. I'll also leave a message for Julia letting her know you've returned. I'm sure she'll pass it on to your guard dogs—sorry, I mean friends." He teased her gently, playful, hoping to provoke a smile.

Her eyebrows twitched as if in response and then her face softened.

Obviously, she hadn't cottoned on to his plan to keep her from fleeing him all over again. He hoped that if her friends found out about her return to the city and the adventures of the past day, they would be keen to contact her, to check on her and that would make her escape all that much more difficult.

A very small smile spread her lips slightly. "Thank you." Her tone was sincere. "I'd really appreciate that."

With his own warm smile, he nodded at her. Things were improving. He could feel he was making headway and Lucy was beginning to relax again.

Tugging her torn dress further around herself, Lucy moved to step back into her room. At the threshold, she turned. "I'll see you at the office tomorrow morning," she told him, her tone strangely reassuring.

Then she was gone, her door closed and locked behind her.

She'd see him tomorrow morning? It was a pledge he hadn't expected her to make, being certain himself that she would do everything in her power to hide from him now that things had gotten…intimate. Yet, he'd hold her to that. Perhaps she wasn't about to run after all.

CHAPTER NINE

The softness of Cal's warm lips had trailed their way below Lucy's belly button. Her breath had caught in her throat at the anticipation of knowing that he was working his way lower. Although she was hot and aching for all of him, desperate for him to enter her, fill her and complete her, she no longer had any control over her actions. She was absolute putty in his hands. She wanted him so badly, wanted his hands all over her, needed his lips on her skin.

Lucy needed more of him, she couldn't get enough, but the material of her dress was in the way. Why had she worn anything to dinner? At this moment, it surely would have made more sense to attend naked—as long as Cal had been naked too.

She licked her lips and felt her thighs press together at the thought of his mouth so close to the part of her that craved his touch the most. Slick and burning for him, Lucy feared she might come at the slightest sensation, the lightest kiss, a delicate stroke.

The slam of a door had her chin slipping off the palm of her hand and toward the top of her desk before she caught herself and opened her eyes.

Steph was staring at her with a look of curious surprise

as Lucy struggled to straighten in her chair.

"What?" She knew it sounded defensive.

With an innocent expression, Steph shook her head. "Nothing."

It was sure to be after nine and Lucy was certain Mia had sent Steph to either offer to include her in their dinner plans or be dragged home with continuous complaints. Everyone else in the office had left hours ago, even Cal, along with Julia, had headed out in the early afternoon to finalize the last of their plans with the approved contractors.

Just as she'd done the last few days, Lucy had hidden in her office all day and when she wasn't hiding, she was relying on text messages from Steph and Mia to warn her when Cal was coming into the building. Every time Cal was about to enter Insight Marketing, Lucy suddenly needed to go out for coffee—even though it was available in the tearoom—lunch—even though she'd brought her own—and to post some very important mail—even though Joseph was the building's resident mailman. Since calling in sick the day after her little interlude at the Cardinal Winery with Cal—although she was more heartsick than physically sick—and being repetitively scolded by Julia for her slackness, Lucy had decided to brave work—but with certain conditions. The main one being avoid Cal at all costs.

Although her friends had made things that little bit easier, aiding her escape whenever they could, her relationship with Julia—and Trent for that matter—was definitely becoming strained. Julia, of course, was desperate for Lucy to do everything in her power to keep the rich client happy, while Trent was quieter than usual, even refraining from his beloved obnoxious comments— which was almost scarily out-of-character for him.

"So?" Steph had made her way farther into the room, her black wide-leg slacks swaying as she rounded the desk and then propped herself on the edge of the desktop.

Ignoring the thoughts of concern that plagued her, Lucy narrowed her eyes at her close friend. *"So?"*

A grin spread across Steph's lips. "What were you daydreaming about?"

For a split second, Lucy felt her eyes widen as the memory of Cal's slow, seductive progress down the bare skin of her stomach flared behind her retinas. She shook her head to shake the thought away and then to answer Steph.

"Nothing." Her tone wasn't as soft and innocent as she hoped it would be.

Steph watched Lucy closely, her grin more knowing now than teasing. "Whatever you say, Lucy-cakes."

Lucy frowned. Damn it, she really was a terrible liar.

With a chuckle, Steph glanced down at the mountains of files that covered Lucy's desk and then back up into Lucy's firm gaze. "I know this is an important project and that we have a very intimidating deadline, but it is a Saturday and we've already worked enough overtime for the week. What do you say you, Mia, and I head out to get some chow?"

A smile tickled the corners of Lucy's mouth. She'd been right about Steph's reasons for entering her office.

"And what happens to me if I say no?"

Steph's eyebrows shot up and she glanced toward the closed glass door at the other side of the room. "Are you crazy?" Her question was poised with limited humor. "Don't let Mia hear you say that word. She'll be in here and dragging you out by your hair if she gets just the slightest whisper of a negative response."

Lucy laughed at the flicker of feigned fear in Steph's eyes. "Oh, okay. You've convinced me," she told her, conceding far too easily.

Steph pretended to breathe a sigh of relief and then grinned triumphantly. "She really threatened that, you know?"

With a tilt of her head, Lucy began gathering her

belongings, putting things needed for home in either her handbag or handy canvas bag. "I don't doubt it. She's such a slave driver."

Nodding in agreement, Steph chuckled. "That's just one of the many things I love about her."

Screwing up her face in pretend disgust, Lucy shoved Steph's shoulder playfully, her fingers pushing against the crisp ivory cotton of her button-down blouse. "Enough of the mushy stuff. I don't want to ruin my appetite." Gathering her bags, she pushed Steph around the desk and toward the office door. "Where are we heading for dinner, anyway?"

"Rosie's."

That answer had Lucy pausing in her exit. She'd assumed they'd be dropping into a restaurant on the way home, maybe even a fast food joint—geez, even a kebab place. She definitely hadn't considered that they'd be heading over to Rosie's at this time of night. This was becoming more obviously a setup by the minute.

"I suppose I don't get a choice in that either."

Pleased with herself, Steph shook her head and then rubbed her hands together, looking wickedly eager in her anticipation. "We're having a girls' night and there's no way you're gonna get out of it."

***

Steph took a long swig of her beer before being the first of them to verbalize a response to the entire dramatic monologue Lucy had just finished.

"Crap." It was a long, breathy, drawn-out syllable that spoke volumes.

Lucy thought it suited the whole situation quite nicely. "Pretty much," she agreed.

They were all gathered around Rosie's modern, white dining table which had a line of half-empty bowls of different salads, roasted vegetables, and homemade fried chicken down the center, as well as numerous glasses, beer and wine bottles—some empty—and the rest of their own dirty dishes. Everyone except Rosie, who'd managed to go casual since she was the only one at home, was still dressed in their professional work clothes and for that reason, Lucy thought that their girl-chat could've easily been mistaken for a dinner meeting had some passerby turned voyeur and glanced through the picture window that led out onto the well-lit street beside them.

"Geez," Mia began. "Lucy, what—" She shook her head as though gathering her thoughts. "What are you going to do?"

Rosie raked a hand through her blonde curls and breathed out a sigh. "She's got to stay away from him."

Mia snorted at that conclusion. "I don't think he's going to stay away from her."

"Are you sure he's not looking for something deeper?" Steph stared at Lucy, her expression more hopeful than her tone.

Lucy nibbled at her fingernails nervously. "It seemed like it in the moment. I really thought there was something between us, something lasting, but then…it just deteriorated. I think he was just taking advantage of the situation. He probably saw it as a way to complete the collection. Sleep with me and then there's only Maddy left—and he won't sleep with her because she's married."

"With a reputation like his, don't be too sure," Mia snipped.

Lucy covered her face with her hands in mortification. "Oh God, I'm such an idiot."

"I don't know." Steph's tone was cautious and critical. "I've seen the look on his face when he checks your empty office or when we tell him you've just popped out of the building. He doesn't look like someone filled with annoyance or disappointment that they won't be able to scratch another name off their screw list. He looks devastated, broken—fearful even. I don't think it's just about sex for him."

When Lucy's hands dropped from her face, she knew that her expression was more hopeful than she wanted it to appear, but the thought that one of her closest friends believed there could be something deeper to Cal's feelings for her made her heart skip a beat.

Could it be possible? Had she just misunderstood the situation? Was it as difficult for Cal as it was for her to admit his feelings? Everything inside her hoped so, but she couldn't be certain. After all, Mia was right, Cal's reputation proved that his love life never revolved around feelings.

As Steph nodded, Mia frowned.

"Lucy," Mia's tone held a tinge of wariness, "Maybe Steph is right. I've seen the look she's talking about. He doesn't look like an asshole. But, unfortunately, that doesn't mean that he's not one."

Rosie chuckled. "With a face like his, how many women would even care?" She lifted her hand sheepishly. "I, for one, would buy a ticket for that ride anytime."

Mia spat out a laugh and then nodded in agreement as Steph rolled her eyes. "He's definitely a handsome honey." Then, as her expression became more serious, she glanced over at Lucy. "He's the type of man who would have women throwing themselves at him daily."

Lucy scoffed as the memory of the overzealous waitress at the winery resurfaced. "You've got no idea," she told them.

"Well," Mia continued her train of thought. "Then why would he need to collect the set of you and your friends if he could have his choice of women, anyway?"

Narrowing her gaze, Lucy considered the question.

"It could be a pride thing." Rosie shrugged. "Maybe he wants to be able to brag about it?"

Steph grunted her disapproval. "Do you really think he'd care about something so trivial? Chances are, he's got a few supermodels as ex-lovers, so why wouldn't he just brag about them?"

Frowning, Rosie offered them all another shrug. "I've got nothing."

Mia stared at Lucy, studying her carefully. "Maybe I'm wrong, Luce. Maybe he does care?"

"Either way," Steph said, as she leaned forward and rested her elbows on the tabletop, "you aren't going to figure it out by chatting to us. There's only one way you can find out if his feelings for you are genuine and that's by talking to him and getting to know him—the person he is now—much better."

Lucy made a whining noise low in her throat. She really hated that idea. It was hard enough for her to stop thinking about him when she wasn't with him, to stop thinking about him touching her, how she felt with his hands on her naked torso, his lips on her skin. How was she ever going to be able to keep her thoughts straight if she was in the same room as him?

Reaching across the table, Lucy placed her hand over Steph's. "Are you sure you can't do some snooping for me?"

Steph smirked, but shook her head.

"I will," Mia piped up excitedly.

"No." Steph's tone was almost scolding. "I think this may be something Lucy has to do on her own."

When Lucy pouted, Mia responded with a quick wink.

Perhaps Lucy wouldn't be running this gauntlet alone after all.

"That means," Steph continued, drawing Lucy's gaze back to hers, "you need to be *available*." As Lucy opened her mouth to protest, Steph silenced her with a swift wave of her hand. "And *that means* you need to be in your office when Cal's in the building."

Sighing resignedly, Lucy gave a curt nod in agreement. "Fine."

With a genial smile, Rosie shrugged. "At least it will get Julia off your back."

Her eyes wide, Mia nodded exaggeratedly. "Yep. She's really got it in for you. She keeps telling me she'd love to fire you for putting her through this farce, but she can't because you're the best exec she's got and she knows it."

"Oi," Steph whined, as she playfully elbowed Mia softly in the ribs. "Who's the best executive?"

As Mia rolled her eyes at her girlfriend's fake grimace, Rosie and Lucy laughed whole-heartedly.

Perhaps, being available to Cal wouldn't be as painful as Lucy expected? After all, she would be at work, where other people could see her, where Julia was counting on her to do her job and keep the peace—maybe she could keep her mind on task? Maybe she wouldn't find Cal so alluring in the workplace environment? Maybe, if she kept her distance, they could form a fruitful working relationship together?

And maybe she could stop fantasizing about what happened the other night, about Cal's lips on hers, his fingers caressing her soft, sensitive skin?

Yeah, fat chance, Lucy thought.

***

Trendy theatergoers milled in and out of the upmarket bar aptly named the Stage Door as the Melbourne Theatre Company next door closed for the night.

"Great show," exclaimed a grey-haired gentleman in a tailored pinstripe suit and ruby cravat as he clasped his hands affectionately on Toby's broad shoulders. "Absolutely tremendous."

Toby nodded in silent appreciation before the man appeared to spot someone at the other end of the bar and then headed deeper into the crowd.

Cal watched as the gentleman met with another cheerful group and they burst into conversation at his appearance.

"Who was that?" Cal asked as he glanced back to Toby,

116

who was perched on the stool beside him at the bar.

Toby's brown-eyed gaze was still intently watching the joyful group as the older gentleman with the ruby cravat signaled once again in his direction. With a quick wave of acknowledgement, Toby instinctively tugged at the indigo hem of his suit jacket and then smoothed his matching velvet lapels. When the man finally turned his back to them, Toby gave Cal his full attention.

"He's the chair on the board of shareholders." He rolled his dark eyes, his thick, black brows rising in fluid motion with the movement and then gave a half-hearted shrug. "Theatre politics. Got to keep the highbrows happy."

Cal nodded. He understood what that was like. His own board was difficult enough to please in the business arena, he couldn't imagine having to also socialize with them as Toby often had to.

"So, your mother told my mother that I have to tell you to call her." Toby's unimpressed tone made the statement sound even more absurd than it already was.

Cal frowned. "She has a phone. She could always call me."

Toby shrugged, indifferently.

Shortly after his father's death, Cal's mother, Charmaine, moved out of their Melbourne penthouse apartment and back to Adelaide to be closer to her siblings and their families. Although he'd promised to visit as often as he could, Cal had only made it to the inner-city mansion he'd bought for her twice in the past three and a half years. If he was honest with himself, he'd barely called her more than half a dozen times since she'd left as well. Besides the fact that he was always extremely busy looking after Hawthorne Incorporated, Cal also wasn't a fan of their conversations anymore. He hadn't settled down, hadn't married, or had children and that was something his mother just didn't quite understand. Cal had even tried to explain to her about his feelings for Lucy, but she hadn't grasped the fact that he couldn't possibly *just find someone else*—Lucy was his *one* and always would be.

After habitually undoing the waist button of his grey suit jacket, Cal made himself more comfortable and leaned his elbows on the clean, dark wood of the bar's countertop. Although the glass of neat scotch that he twirled slightly in his fingers was helping to calm his nerves a little, it wasn't exactly doing the trick. He still felt itchy, uneasy, and his legs thrummed with vibration as though he needed to move—but he'd been moving all day.

When he hadn't been looking for Lucy—as he had every day for the last three days—searching the entire office building for her, Cal had been out, focused on organizing preparation for the structural work that was to be done to the Gold Coast property. He and Julia had finalized the last of the plans for the improvements this afternoon and he had run everything past Paul Gillies, the reliable hotel manager who had been loyal to the Calypso—and the Hawthorne family—for over twenty years. Luckily, his late father had had the foresight to modernize the kitchens, bathrooms, balconies, and the internal elevators a little over ten years ago. Phillip Hawthorne had also been vigilant in ensuring the whole building regularly underwent structural examinations as he always had with all his properties. Cal's father had never been one to do things half-cocked, it was just one of the many things Cal had admired about him.

As well as refining the front facade of the Calypso, Cal had hired contractors to create a game room where the bar lounge had been, redesign and landscape the pool, revamp the Great Hall, paint the entire premises inside and out, and then clean all glass, including windows and balcony rails. All internal and external furnishings were to be delivered and arranged over the twentieth and twenty-first of April, in just over two weeks.

Cal was expecting a great deal from his team, both the people at Insight Marketing who were about to start shopping around the Calypso's new advertising campaign to the media and all the exceptional contractors he'd hired at last minutes' notice. Although he was paying them all double or triple their usual requirements in order to get the job done swiftly—and correctly—he was still impressed that so many people had agreed to his high demands. As of tomorrow, there would be over one hundred and fifty people working on the Gold Coast property at any one time. Cal just prayed everything would go as smoothly as was necessary.

Suddenly, the bouncing of his right knee, the incessant fidgeting of his vibrating limbs freed him from his thoughts. He placed a firm hand on the fabric of his grey dress pants, forcing his knee to calm its rhythm.

"Okay, I've just got to ask." Toby had turned on the bar stool next to him so that he was facing Cal directly. There was a curious, nearly suspicious smile curling his full lips. "You mentioned you finally caught up with Lucy a few days ago. I'm assuming that's what has got you all twisted up inside?"

Cal stared at Toby and fought to keep the feeling of utter dejection from showing on his face. "More than that actually."

Eyes widening, Toby's dark eyebrows rose with excitement. "Oh, really?"

Sighing, Cal finished his scotch and signaled the bartender to serve up another. Cal swore as he remembered the look on Lucy's face, the tears in her eyes and then the anger and hurt that filled her when she moved to leave the room, to leave him.

The bartender placed another glass of aged scotch whisky in front of him and Cal drank it down like an ordinary tequila shot. As the smooth alcohol burned warmly, enjoyably along the back of his throat, Cal lowered the glass back to the hard, dark wood of the countertop.

"I think I've messed up, Toby." It was said so quietly, Cal wondered if Toby would even understand.

His expression becoming serious, Toby rested a tanned hand supportively on Cal's strong shoulder. "It can't be that bad, cuz. You may be a fool when it comes to all things lovey-dovey, but you're a good guy. Whatever you've stuffed up, you can fix it."

Cal shook his head. "I'm not so sure, Tobe. I really took it too far this time. I'd just found her again, just got my Lucy back and had hoped to win her over slowly, proving to her that I truly care about her, but then I went and screwed everything up. I lost control and threw myself at her." Cal dropped his face into his hands, his voice becoming even more despondent. "Stripped her." He shook his head again, his large hands still covering his face. "I don't think I'm going to get another chance."

Sighing deeply, his face stricken with pain for his beloved cousin, Toby ran his fingers through his wavy, black hair. "Have you told her that you're in love with her?" His voice was hoarse, pained as though he was fearing the worst.

Shaking his head once more, Cal lifted his face from his hands and stared at Toby. "How can I? I'm pretty sure she still hates me."

Toby's expression narrowed in exasperation and he dropped his hand from Cal's shoulder. "Well, I'm pretty sure she wouldn't have gotten naked with you if she hated you."

Cal offered Toby a grimace. Who was he kidding? Of course, Lucy could still hate him. Toby hadn't seen that look in her eyes. The fear, the anger. At the time, Cal had questioned whether or not that had been more for herself than for him, that she was afraid of her own feelings for him, her *love* for him. But now, after days of continued rejection, getting no more than a polite, but brief email or text message in reply to his own and never once crossing her path in person, yet being told she'd just popped out of the office and would be back soon, Cal was definitely beginning to feel as though he'd lost Lucy for real this time. How could he possibly apologize, how could he possibly win her over if he couldn't even meet with her in person?

"Cal," Toby began, his tone composed, but reproachful, "I think you need to talk to Lucy and this time, actually tell her how you feel about her."

Cal narrowed his eyes. It was all well and good for Toby to tell him what to do, but Toby didn't know just how difficult a task that was—for many reasons. "How can I tell her that I love her, when she won't even see me anymore?"

This time it was Toby who frowned. "Aren't you working together trying to fix up the Calypso?"

Nodding briefly, Cal quirked an eyebrow as though in challenge. "Yep, but for the last three days I haven't seen hair or luscious hide of her in the office or out of it. She won't return my calls." He pulled his smartphone free of his jacket pocket and placed it on the bar counter, pressing the screen a few times before pushing the device closer to Toby. "And all I get in reply are short emails or these kinds of text messages."

Toby glanced down at the brightly lit screen of the phone. "Thanks for your call," he read the message aloud. "I'm currently busy working on the Calypso's ad campaign with the other execs. Please contact Julia if you need something urgently. Lucy." As he looked back up at Cal and pushed the phone back toward him, Toby breathed in deeply through gritted teeth, making a harsh sound. "Crap, Cal. That's pretty cold."

"You're telling me," Cal agreed as he closed his eyes in an effort to ignore the clenching ache deep in his chest.

"I still think you should tell her."

Cal's gaze flicked back to Toby at his firm instruction. "You can't be serious?" Feeling himself fill with a burning annoyance, Cal thinned his lips. "How can I tell her when she won't talk to me, won't even see me?"

A small, sly smile pulled at the corners of Toby's

mouth. "You don't give her a choice," he said flatly.

Cal's expression contorted in a mixture of anger and confusion. "What?"

Toby smiled cunningly. "If you can't find her at the office, you can find her at home. Tell her that. I'm willing to bet that she'll be available in the office from that moment on."

His expression softening, Cal thought about Toby's suggestion. Sure, it was a bit underhanded, but so was hiding from him for days. If Lucy could play her own game, then Cal could play his.

Cal's smoky-blue gaze met Toby's dark brown eyes. They shared a grin.

"You're on," Cal told his cousin.

"Great." Toby rubbed his hands together victoriously. "I think it's time we get another round and you fill me in on all the dirty details of your lewd, naked evening with our Lucy."

Scowling playfully, Cal held his index finger up between them as though pointing out a problem with the last remark. "*My* Lucy," he corrected sharply, but impishly. "And don't you forget that, little cousin."

Toby laughed heartily. "C'mon," he teased. "She's the sister I never had. I deserve a little ownership."

Cal's eyes widened at Toby's response and he chuckled. "You know, she'd likely punch us both if she ever heard us claiming any *ownership* over her, right?"

"Right," Toby agreed with a stiff nod as his hand unconsciously moved to rub his right shoulder as though in memory of an old injury. "She did have a wicked right hook when she used to run around playing Wonder Woman."

CHAPTER TEN

Making herself available had seemed like a pretty good plan to Lucy, even if it had been Steph who'd suggested it. Yet there seemed to be one key thing missing from their important plan—Cal.

For the last few days, Cal had been MIA. First, he was whisked off by Julia to another meeting of the contractors—this time to confirm details regarding changes to the Gold Coast property's pool—then, the Insight Marketing team had been informed that he'd needed to spend a few days at Hawthorne Incorporated to finalize yet another acquisition to the empire's property portfolio.

If Lucy hadn't known better, she would have wondered if Cal was now *avoiding her*. But that was ridiculous—wasn't it?

It seemed strange to her now that she'd spent so much time hiding from him, avoiding him, that when he seemed to be doing the same it actually began to worry her. For some reason, she kept questioning if she'd truly ruined her chances to get to know him better, to get to know the new Cal. What if she really had stuffed things up by rejecting him so blatantly? It actually scared her. She'd only just gotten him back. She didn't want to lose him now, not before finding out how he really felt about her and not after what happened the other night. Lucy didn't know if she could survive a life without the promise of his touch, without hoping to once again be lost to her desires in his arms. Even though she still couldn't be sure of his intentions, she realized now—maybe too late—that she, at the very least, wanted to find out what they were.

Lucy was sick of sitting around in her office waiting and procrastinating, staring at the same document that still required the same proofread that she'd started over two hours ago. She really needed to do something, to keep busy and stop her mind from going over and over different scenarios in her head. Of course, Cal was coming back in and of course, he couldn't possibly avoid her forever—even though she had done a pretty good job of hiding from him for nearly half their lives. It was time for her to stop stressing about mistakes she might have made and focus on something current that she had firm control over.

Lucy glanced over her desk. Piles of paper, some with colorful sticky notes attached, stretched from corner to corner like a white, miniature, mountainous landscape. Her computer monitor was pushed to the far-left side and her keyboard perched in front of it atop a peak of colored plastic folders. To the right sat Lucy's in and out trays, but only one overflowed with various files and dull, buff-colored manila folders, while the other contained a single lonely file.

She had meant to pass that file on to Rosie or one of the assistants in her own team to have it photocopied in triplicate before filing a copy, but she'd planned to do that once she'd proofread the document that still sat before her. Seeing an opportunity to escape the suffocation of her office and the incessant procrastination she just couldn't seem to shake while sitting there, Lucy grabbed the completed file and headed for her office door.

Sure, the photocopy room was just another dreary space like that of her office—with no sign of Cal in sight—but at least in there she could keep her hands occupied, actually doing something if she found her mind wandering again.

Lucy had made it halfway through photocopying the document before the door to the small private room opened. Although her mind reasoned that it was just another work colleague, maybe even Steph or Mia, Lucy's heart did an excited, little flip-flop in her chest at the sudden hope that maybe, just maybe, it was Cal.

When Trent took one look at her and stepped inside, closing the door carefully behind him, Lucy was almost pleased to see him. He had barely spoken to her since her outing with Cal to the Cardinal Winery and she was beginning to feel anxious about his sudden quietness.

"Hey there." Her cheerful voice pierced through the sudden silence of the room as she paused in her photocopying.

The room itself was rather small, not exactly claustrophobic, but only big enough to a fit a large, multifunction photocopier at each end and an expensive, specialist A3 printer in the middle.

His expression hard, Trent strode the few steps toward her. As usual, he presented a handsome figure in his fitted black slacks and tight mustard business shirt. Even his jet-black hair was perfectly slicked in place. His stylish appearance had Lucy questioning her own.

Although Lucy had made a substantial effort to look a mixture of professional and sexy over the last few days in her hope of seeing Cal, today—whether out of hopelessness or laziness—she had dialed both down a few notches. Her knee-length draped skirt was black and so too, was her short-sleeved cotton cardigan. Only her white silk camisole had a wisp of color in the form of a floral design along the hem. She hadn't even bothered with heels today, instead wearing boring, but comfortable black flats and she was pretty sure—without looking at her reflection—that her hair needed a good brush through too.

With that thought, Lucy's left hand went to the side of her dark, straight, shoulder-length hair and she made a half-hearted effort to smooth it even straighter.

Even though Trent's expression remained firm, Lucy offered him a small smile as he reached her, and she tried mentally to quell the uneasy feeling that was building in her gut.

"Trent?" Her tone surprised her, sounding almost fearful.

Still, he remained silent. He was staring at her, then at his hands, then back up at her, his jaw clenching with each minute movement.

Just over a foot away now, Trent suddenly seemed too close to her. Lucy began to wish the photocopier had been between them. Unable to hide her feeling of discomfort, she took a step back from him and ended up nearly flush against the cold, cream wall behind her.

"Trent? Are you okay?" The words slipped out before she could think them through. Trent was not a person who liked to be asked that question when angry.

His dark green eyes bore into hers, before he closed them and a deep, steadying breath escaped his lips. When he looked at her again, his expression softened slightly.

"Lucy, I've been trying to find the right time to talk to you." He spoke slowly as though trying to retain control over the darkness Lucy had seen in his gaze a moment ago.

"Okay," Lucy said, sounding more like she was trying to pacify a man with a gun than just agreeing to what was said. "Is now the right time?"

Instinctively, she crossed her arms over her chest as though trying to put some sort of physical barrier between them.

Trent's eyebrows furrowed tightly, and he breathed out a loud, frustrated sigh. "I think so." He shook his head. "I don't know."

His expression appeared pained and Lucy had a sudden urge to comfort him. Her arms relaxed over her chest, but she fought the impulse she had to reach out to touch him on the shoulder reassuringly.

"It's okay, Trent." Lucy spoke soothingly. "You can tell me whatever you need to."

Abruptly, a strong hand flew past her face and landed solidly on the wall behind her. The sudden movement scared Lucy causing her to press herself back against the wall as Trent leaned in over her.

"Lucy," Trent breathed, his head lowered to hers, his mouth so close she could smell the remnants of his mid-morning coffee on his breath. "I want you to stay away from *him*."

Lucy swallowed nervously and forced herself to look away from him, tilting her head to the side. "Stay away from whom, Trent?" Her voice was breathy, but she found the courage to finish more strongly. "You're really starting to freak me out. Maybe you were right, this isn't the best time."

"No." Trent's voice was firm and defiant. "I think now is perfect."

Fearful and with her heartbeat racing, Lucy's arms stiffened over her chest until she felt as though she were hugging herself. How had she gotten herself into this situation?

As Lucy silently weighed her options, wondering whether or not she could be quick enough to dart around him, Trent's head lowered and she felt the warmth of his breath blow through the strands of her hair to tickle her neck. Still, he was careful not to touch her.

"I know about the winery," he said sharply.

Lucy held her breath. Had one of the girls told Trent about what had happened? Surely not. The Girl Code had to count for something.

"He's just using you, Lucy. You need to know that he doesn't really care about you." Trent sighed again as though releasing further frustration.

Lucy's hair swayed against the delicate skin of her neck and she thought that for a second, Trent had caressed a strand between his fingers—but she wasn't brave enough to turn her face to see.

She took a shaky breath. "You might be right," she told him, both in an effort to appease him and because she had questioned the same issue herself for a long time.

"It would be best for you to keep away from him."

Although Trent's tone was almost caring, non-threatening, Lucy couldn't help but take it negatively. It was bad enough that he had her cowering below him, using his height and bulk to intimidate her. She had even felt it best to ignore the defamatory remarks about Cal because she had yet to have real evidence to prove them otherwise. But to threaten her, to remove *her* free will—even if he was just implying it—well, that was going a little too far.

"Sorry?" she questioned him, her anger subduing her fear just enough for her to turn her head toward him. "Did you just threaten me?"

Trent pulled his head back to look into her eyes. He looked surprised. "Lucy—no—"

Lucy glared at him, fury overwhelming her. She felt as though the exasperation of the last few days, the distress and worry that had consumed her with each second that had passed without seeing Cal was finally culminating in this moment, in this feeling of rage.

"Who the hell do you think you are, Trent?" Her voice was low and menacing. Pushing herself free of the rigid wall behind her, Lucy unclasped her arms and then pointed her index finger at Trent accusingly. "Going on a couple of coffee dates with me doesn't give you the right to tell me who I can and cannot see."

Grimacing, Trent took a step backward, dropping his hand from the wall, before Lucy's finger could poke him in the chest. "I just wanted to warn you," he told her, his voice gentle and sincere. "I didn't mean to upset you."

"Yes, you did," Lucy snapped. "I'm sure you already know that Cal and I have a history, and I know all about his womanizing reputation, so what is there to warn me about? Why else did you come in here? What else were you planning to tell me?"

Trent looked away, his look of concern disappearing. When his dark green eyes returned her gaze, his expression appeared assured and determined. "You have to know that I care about you, Lucy. That we've grown to be more than just friends."

Lucy fought the urge to roll her eyes as her fury began to fade. Sure, she thought Trent was reasonably good-looking, if a little too perfectly preened—and his facial features were a little too harsh—but they'd barely made it beyond first base and that was only because one of their coffee dates had happened to have a unisex bathroom.

As she was searching her brain for a nice way of letting him down without telling him that he was essentially a romantic fill-in, the door to the photocopy room opened.

His expression contorting, obviously annoyed by the interruption, Trent turned away from Lucy to glare at the intruder.

"Lucy, Rosie told me you were—" Cal paused mid-sentence, obviously noticing the tension in the room. Narrowing his stare, he gave Trent a fierce, tight-lipped smile, which seemed to promise grievous bodily harm if his adversary stepped out of line. "Clearly I'm interrupting."

"You bet your ass you are," Trent growled.

The brief excitement that made Lucy's heartbeat quicken when she'd first seen Cal quickly diminished as Trent took a menacing step toward him. Irritated once more and concerned she may be about to witness a fight that could potentially destroy a photocopier, Lucy hurried forward and around Trent.

Cal slipped farther into the room. His body language

became protective as his shoulders squared in his stylish merlot-colored jacket and his chest puffed up beneath his eggshell white business shirt.

"Cool it," Lucy told them, but her authoritative gaze was locked on her volatile colleague.

Trent's ominous scowl flicked to Lucy, and he watched her carefully for what felt like a long time, before straightening brusquely. "Fine. Remember what I said." He walked toward her, leaning close to her as he passed. "I'll be in my office when you're ready to continue our conversation." His glare was icy as he took a wide berth around Cal and then exited the room.

Cal was quick to close the door behind him. Once they were finally alone, Cal's stiff posture relaxed as he turned back to face Lucy. "Do I need to have a chat with Julia to see about getting that asshole fired?"

Lucy hugged her arms around her waist. "No." She shook her head as she thought it over. "He's just been a little off recently. If I had to guess, I'd say it was because of you."

"No, kidding." His chuckle sounded jaded.

Cal held her gaze, his eyes searching hers.

"I'll be okay," she told him quickly, seeing a look of concern contort his handsome features. "He just surprised me is all."

Cal frowned. "It looks as though he's done more than that."

Shrugging, Lucy glanced away from him and wandered aimlessly toward the other end of the small room. "We've had a couple of minor dates—just coffee really. Trent's got it into his head that we've got something special together—never mind that I'm not really feeling it." Lucy stopped walking and faced him. "Sorry, I didn't mean to overshare. It's nothing really. I've just got to find a way to tell him otherwise."

Cal's gaze narrowed almost suspiciously. "For any reason I should know?"

Lucy swallowed nervously and then forced a smile. "So, it's been a while since I've seen you around the office?"

He raised an eyebrow. "I could say the same thing to you."

She lowered her head and looked at the floor as she tried to muffle the anxious giggle that fought free of her mouth. "Okay, bad choice of subject," she told him.

Cal took the few steps toward her, closing the space between them in an instant. Catching his movement out the corner of her eye, Lucy skipped free of him at the last minute. She turned her back to him and pretended to be interested in the photocopier, the opposite one to the device she'd been actively using moments before. Lucy could sense Cal move up behind her.

"Are we okay, Luce?" His voice sounded hoarse.

She nodded enthusiastically, then wondered whether the movement had been more to convince herself than to prove to him that everything between them was all right. "Yeah. I guess I'm still a bit flustered about before with Trent."

Taking a steadying breath for courage, Lucy spun to face him. She smiled again, but she could feel that it lacked sincere luster.

Cal's smoky-blue eyes flickered with hurt as his expression furrowed with worry. "I'm sorry I let everything get so out-of-control at the winery. I hadn't meant for things to move so quickly." His grimace was full of self-deprecation. "But, Luce—" Cal's eyes brightened as he said her nickname. "You have to know that everything that happened that night meant the absolute world to me. I may not have expected them to happen so soon, but I wouldn't take them back for anything. Kissing you—" He sighed as though at the thought. "God, touching you—it was everything I've always wanted since I met you all those years ago."

Lucy's eyes widened as her heart did a somersault in her chest, making her stomach feel as though she'd just started down the steep descent of a rollercoaster. But it was all too soon. She still hadn't gotten to know this new Cal, to discover whether these feelings he was willing to offer up so freely were for her alone or for her right now. She needed more time to find out whether the Cal in front of her might be mature and honest enough to trust with her heart.

Cal's gaze narrowed as though in response to her silence and he moved to speak again, but Lucy stopped him, raising her hand between them.

"I know, Cal." She stared deep into his eyes, willing him to understand while she spoke slowly, as though that would make what she had to say less hurtful. "I know. I'm not saying that I didn't feel the same, but for the moment, I just need everything to slow down."

Cal's jaw tensed and he reached out to her, his hand moving toward her shoulder. Again, Lucy stopped him, grabbing his hand with her own. His large palm felt warm and sturdy beneath the smallness of hers. His frown deepened.

"I like you." She returned his frown as she struggled to find the right words. "I like what I know of you so far—of this new Cal, but I need more. I need us just to work together, to get to know each other properly, to become friends again first and then maybe—" Lucy's voice trailed off as she realized she wasn't quite ready to define what she hoped might be their future relationship.

For what felt like an eternity, Cal just looked at her, his gaze analyzing her face and then his expression softened. "Does that mean I'll actually get to see you around the office from now on? That maybe you'll even work together with me?"

Lucy nodded, feeling her features hardening in suspicion. "That would be the idea, yes."

A mischievous smirk spread his lips. "So, that means I don't have to threaten you with the old *I know where you live—now*—thing to convince you to spend time with me?

You'll be ready and willing on your own accord?"

An exasperated sigh escaped her lips as Lucy rolled her eyes and snatched her hand back from his. "Obviously, I was wrong. You're still a jerk." Although her words sounded sharp, Lucy knew they were only half-hearted.

Cal might have been used to getting what he wanted, throwing money at someone and having them jump or playing the intimidation card and watching people cower, but those weren't things that would work on her and he was sure to know that by now. He was just lucky that this time, what she needed right now and what he was happy with for the moment happened to mesh. It was what he wanted in the long term that still had her guessing.

"Don't be like that," he all but cooed to her as his hand, now free from hers, moved to its previously desired destination.

Lucy resisted the need to push his strong hand from her shoulder. She glared up at him, the corners of her mouth itching to return his inane smirk. "Did I say that I *liked* you? Yeah, that had to be a slip of the tongue."

Cal chuckled and his hand crept higher, his fingers gently caressing the soft material of her cardigan. Yet, Lucy felt it lower as though there were no barrier between his touch and the skin of her shoulder and then deeper, from the tight tips of her nipples to the spark of a tempting tingle at her feminine core. She was suddenly very aware of how close he was. They'd been mere inches from each other the entire time, the curves of her slender figure so close to melting against the hard lines of his.

Cal leaned down just a little, his full lips nearing hers. "I may be a jerk," he whispered, "but you like me, anyway."

Lucy meant to snort at his blatant cockiness, but as she went to do so, Cal's wandering fingers reached the bare skin of her neck and instead, it became a sharp intake of breath and then Lucy was lost for words.

Cal chuckled again and Lucy knew her expression must have given her away. Of course, her eyes had widened at the shock of electricity that had passed through her at his touch and of course, her face had heated as her thoughts had turned sensual. Although, a small part of her was screaming for control, wanting to regain the upper hand, the rest of her was focused on the sensation flowing through her, the flame of desire that had ignited and now coursed through her veins craving even more.

She caught herself staring at his mouth, thinking of the kisses they shared not that long ago. When she forced her gaze back to his, she noticed Cal's attention was focused intently on her own lips. The hunger inside her grew and the tip of her tongue snuck out to lick her lower lip. Cal's eyes widened and his blue-grey eyes shot back to hers, clearly darkened by his own desire.

Her heart beat rapidly in her chest, almost painfully as her excitement built. Her skin felt so sensitive, it nearly ached. She wanted to reach out to touch him, lean up to kiss him, but she couldn't move. Lucy breathed out a slow breath in an effort to calm her speedy heartbeat.

All of a sudden, Cal's fingers stopped their gentle caress on her neck and time seemed to stop with them. An instant passed, a lifetime, and then his mouth covered hers. As he kissed her, devouring her, his tongue probing, dancing with her own, his body melded with hers, their forms becoming one as she fit perfectly against him.

Lost in the wonder of their embrace, her hands stroked the firmness of his broad chest and then up over his shoulders to rest behind his neck and in the silkiness of his sandy blond hair. When the frolic of his soft tongue became even more passionate, Lucy felt herself moan low in her throat. With a groan of his own, Cal pressed against her, the iron rod of his confined erection a weighty pressure below her bellybutton. His warm hand still cupped her neck below her ear, keeping her close, while the other had found a happy home on the roundness of her derrière.

His lips left hers and he nibbled at the sensitive skin of

her neck. Lucy tried to breathe, but all she could muster were sudden gasps and weak little whimpers. It was overwhelming, yet she still needed more. The feeling of Cal's hot breath against the damp skin of her throat sent the tingle of goosebumps down her body. As her insides quivered, craving more, she moved her hips, rubbing against the rock-hard length of him. Cal groaned again and his mouth returned to hers. He nibbled at her lower lip, sucking it into his mouth before sending his tongue searching deeper inside her, stroking her whole mouth, her teeth, her tongue.

Then his hand slipped from its possessive hold below her ear and made its way down to join the other, resting on the adjacent cheek of her curvy bottom. With his grip firm, he pressed her harder against him and then groaned hoarsely into her mouth. In a quick movement, he lifted her, hands securely under her rump and then she was seated on the photocopier, Cal's hands caressing the top of her thighs.

Lucy heard herself make a small, startled cry as she landed on the uneven plastic of the copying machine's lid, but it wasn't enough to distract her from her desires. Her hands left the safety of their posts and instead explored the muscular figure beneath the starchy fabric of Cal's merlot-colored jacket. The hem of her skirt lifted and she felt his fingers push the dark material higher, removing the restriction it posed and baring the smoothness of her pale thighs. She gasped as she felt him press himself against the moist center of her and then his fingers were there, stroking, touching and her toes curled as the yearning inside her built.

Lucy's lips left his as her head fell back loosely, her mind spellbound by the experience. She wanted him now, needed to feel him inside her. She didn't care where they were or who might see. She was desperate for him, intoxicated by him as though she had always belonged to him—and he had always been hers.

Cal's soft lips found her neck again, kissing the length of her throat and then along her jaw. As his mouth reached Lucy's ear and another surge of goosebumps traveled down her body, his fingers poised to slip beneath the fabric of her black silk panties. A gasp caught in her throat.

The click of the door to the photocopier room caused them both to freeze.

"Oh, crap! Sorry." Mia's tone was high-pitched with embarrassment as it pierced the muffled peace of their intimacy.

It was instantly followed by the louder click of the door being shut quickly.

Lucy could hear the quiet clip-clop of Mia's heels outside as she hurried away down the hall. Slowly, she lifted her head, Cal appeared to do the same, and they caught each other's gaze.

Cal's expression contorted with a mixture of innocence and embarrassment. "I guess this wasn't what you meant when you said you wanted to take things slow?"

Lucy stared up at him, at the concern and helplessness in his wide eyes and at his anxious frown. She tried to stop herself, to control that final, inappropriate desire, but she just couldn't—she laughed.

CHAPTER ELEVEN

It had been an arduous week for Cal, full of teleconferences with contractors in Queensland, review meetings regarding the current live advertising campaigns for the Calypso with the Insight Marketing team, an assortment of necessary phone calls from Hawthorne Incorporated and a number of brief, but very enjoyable, coffee, lunch and dinner breaks which just happened to include his favorite person—Lucy.

Even though he hadn't been able to eat and chat with Lucy at every opportunity, for the most part, he took every advantage offered to him. Most days, they went to get their morning coffee together at the Pink Leaf, a specialized coffee and tea boutique across the street from the office. The same coffee place Lucy had admitted that she and Trent had visited previously. Although it irked Cal to know that Lucy and Trent had shared a kiss or two in the quaint bohemian café, he took great pride in knowing that Lucy had chosen him to share her future experiences with, rather than his angry, self-involved rival.

Cal had been lucky enough to avoid that prick Trent during his time in the office and had done his best to keep Lucy away from him wherever possible. He'd especially made sure that she'd never made it into Trent's office as he'd previously asked, to have them continue the conversation he'd started with her in the photocopy room. It unnerved Cal to think about what had happened and what might have happened between them in that room alone together. He'd seen the look on Lucy's face, noticed how shaken she was by the whole encounter and knew that he would do everything he could to protect her from that sociopathic asshole. Cal just wished she'd let him speak to Julia about the incident and get the dickhead fired, but she claimed that he was good at his job and hadn't really done anything wrong. It took a lot of effort on his part to let the issue go, but Cal did as she asked and focused, instead, on the thrill of spending more time with her.

As for socializing at lunch time, it had usually been in the busy office lunchroom or the building's bustling designated cafeteria. While other staff often joined them, including some of Lucy's friendlier colleagues, there had still been instances when Cal and Lucy had managed to share further quality time alone together, discovering more about each other and who they were now after fourteen years of separation. As Lucy had also requested, Cal had done his best to keep his distance, trying to focus on improving their friendship only. It had been difficult, painful even when he wished desperately to touch her, just to place his hand in hers, but he had survived it.

The few dinners Lucy had allowed Cal to attend had mainly included dining with her close-knit group of girlfriends from the Insight Marketing office. Even though he'd initially felt somewhat intimidated by the experience, fearful that if they didn't approve of him or his treatment of Lucy, he'd be cast out no matter what price he was willing to pay Julia—or them, Cal had quickly discovered that they were an easy-going bunch and much more accepting than he'd expected. It was a pleasure to realize that they all had a similar sense of humor to him and that their love for Lucy and each other made them a unique sort of family unit, a family of friends to which he could easily see himself becoming a part.

During the week, Cal had joined them twice to eat out, once for Chinese and then Italian. They'd ordered Indian into the office on Wednesday as Steph and Lucy had wanted to stay late to evaluate the audience ratings of the Calypso's new television ad and tonight, Cal had actually been invited to Steph and Mia's flat in East Melbourne for homemade pizza and beer.

While Rosie and Mia were in the adjoining lounge room sorting out what music would be best suited to the atmosphere of the evening, Steph was directing Cal and Lucy in the kitchen, getting them to organize plates and cutlery while she adjusted the temperature on the oven. In front of them, on the glossy, stone-flecked top of the kitchen's central island, an assortment of different pizza toppings had already been prepared. There were plates of pepperoni, salami, prosciutto, and grilled chicken. A number of bowls full of fresh, colorful vegetables, as well as small bunches of basil and rocket, fresh and sundried tomatoes, and black and green olives. Blocks of cheddar and parmesan sat open next to a plate arranged with large balls of mozzarella and bocconcini waiting to be grated and sliced, and lastly, a large glass bowl of what Steph referred to her as famous spicy tomato pizza sauce was placed right in the center.

After handing Lucy a ball of homemade pizza dough from the refrigerator, Steph excused herself to go help the others sort through the extensive music collection.

"If I don't go check on them," Steph muttered to Lucy on her way out of the room, "Rosie's bound to choose the Spice Girls or something even more inappropriate like the soundtrack from *Titanic*."

Lucy chuckled and Cal gave her a quizzical look.

"What was that all about?" As the question left his lips, Cal remembered something Steph had said to Rosie about picking music for the masses, not for a nineties school disco.

Lucy shrugged nonchalantly as she unwrapped the plastic that had protected the dough during its stay in the fridge and then plopped it on the flour-covered breadboard in front of them. "Steph's just concerned for our auditory health."

Cal's furrowed brows softened and then he nudged Lucy softly with his shoulder. "I liked the Spice Girls."

She looked up at him, the corners of her small smile twitching as though in surprise—or challenge. "You liked watching me dance to the Spice Girls. There's a difference."

Cal felt his grin widen to become large, white, and toothy. "Is there?" He purposely made his tone innocent.

With a short giggle, Lucy elbowed him playfully in the ribs. "Shut up and help me roll out this dough."

As he moved even closer to her, pushing up the rolled sleeves of his blue cotton business shirt, Cal felt as though his smile was almost beaming out of him. He'd been thrilled when they'd invited him to dinner, partly because he was keen to get to know Lucy's friends better and have them approve of him, and partly because Cal had known that he'd get to spend some more time with Lucy.

Even standing so close to her had sent his heart racing and had caused his chest to become tight and full of anticipation and excitement. The smell of her fruity perfume mixed with the sweet lingering scent of her soap and shampoo had made his heart ache with longing and his groin throb with desire. He was doing all he could to control his building erection, but with the warmth of her soft body so close to his and all those luscious curves just a breath away, Cal was really struggling.

It was torture, just as it had been each time they had been alone over the past week. Although his self-control had been substantial at the beginning, each encounter had worn him down just a little more to the point that his instincts were starting to threaten to take over and do whatever they wanted once the perfect opportunity arose. A tiny part of him, possibly the final shred of his sensibility, was beginning to wish for Steph to return in fear that this very moment may be it.

"Are you actually going to help me or are you just going to stand there?" Lucy's sweet voice brought his attention back into the room.

Realizing that he'd just been staring at the rise of her pert breasts beneath the almost sheer fabric of her rose-pink blouse for heaven-knew how long, Cal quickly flicked his gaze back to the task at hand. Lucy had started trying to roll the pizza dough mound into a flat, circular shape, but the coldness of the dough had made the job a tad harder than normal.

"Here," Cal said as he gently placed his hands over hers on the ends of the wooden rolling pin.

Making certain he didn't crush her fingers with the movement, Cal used his strength to push just that little bit harder on the dough, flattening it with each glide of the rolling pin. Once the dough had been sufficiently molded into a rough pizza shape, Cal paused, the utensil in the center. He knew he should release his hold on Lucy's hands, but it was taking all his willpower to ignore the sensitive position he'd just put himself in. In his swift move to help her, he had become acutely aware of the fact that his body was now flush against hers. Automatically, he'd even slipped one hand beneath her right arm to grasp the furthest end of the rolling pin, something which, in hindsight, was definitely a dangerous idea, since his upper arm was now rubbing against the firm warmth of her right breast and his face was now much too close to hers.

While Cal stared at the flattened dough on the breadboard, trying desperately to steady his breathing and not turn his head to look at her, he felt the quick rise and fall of Lucy's plump chest squishing against him as she breathed. Her rapid breathing told him that she too, was

141

struggling with their proximity, but that she was doing her best to hide it.

Just the thought of her being as hot for him as he was for her, desiring his touch as he craved hers, was enough to remove the last of Cal's inhibitions. He had a second to feel the surge of sensation in his groin, to feel the fiery lust rip through him, and then he was on her. His hands were off the rolling pin and on Lucy's waist, pulling her against him, before either one of them had time for another breath. Instincts rode over the remaining tiny shred of sense that desperately tried to remind him of their current location and that the whole thing wasn't a good idea. Somewhere in his subconscious, Cal noted Lucy's surprised expression, but still he lowered his head and captured her mouth with his. He knew his kiss was rough and possessive, full of want and need, but he didn't care. As Lucy moaned, her body crushed against his, her lips parting, giving in to the demanding stroke of his eager tongue, Cal's hands slipped down from the security of her waist, caressing her soft form until they wrapped solidly around the plush roundness of her backside.

Cal groaned as he held her against him, his solid erection grinding into her. He felt Lucy's hands smooth over his shirt-covered skin to grasp at the broad muscles of his back, her sharp fingernails trying to dig into him greedily as though desiring him closer, harder. It was all too much for him. He needed her now. He'd waited patiently for over a week, only sharing the briefest of nonsexual touches, even though he was frantic to have her, longing to be inside her, to have her wrapped around him, to be breathing her into him, his soul claiming hers. He wanted to have her bare flesh in his hands, to feel that velvet skin beneath his fingers. Cal needed her out of those tight, black pants—now!

As his hands moved to slip between them, beginning to force their bodies apart very slightly, Lucy almost yipped in protest—then the music started.

It was the slow, gentle tones of an unfamiliar indie band, but with an enchanting melody and a saccharine drawl of a female singer.

Lucy froze in his arms and Cal's eyes flew open. He stared into the horrified glint in her bright blue eyes and released her immediately. When her arms dropped limply to her sides, he noticed the telltale signs of their passion in the swelling of her full lips and the flushed pink of her cheeks. He felt his expression harden with concern. What had he done?

"I hope you don't mind some ambient indie music." Steph's footsteps announced her entry into the room. "Mia's Julia Holter album was the strict compromise over the Christina Aguilera album Rosie had stuffed in her purse."

As Steph neared the kitchen's island she paused. It took Cal an unusually long time to drag his gaze from Lucy's, then turn to face Steph.

"It's all good," he said, even though his tone was less than convincing.

Steph's eyebrows furrowed and she cast a glance at Lucy and then back to Cal. She looked as concerned as he felt inside.

"Did I miss something?" She looked at Lucy again. "You okay, Luce?"

With a deep breath, Lucy spun to face her. Cal noticed the firmness of her belly pressing into the cool stone of the benchtop as though giving her something stable to lean against while her legs appeared unsteady.

Shaking her head, her swollen lips spread to form a small smile. "No. I'm fine."

Steph looked at her closely. Her astute hazel eyes seemed to take in every aspect of Lucy's disturbed countenance. After an instant, a grin formed and she glanced back over at Cal.

"You know you should put a sock on the door if you want some privacy," Steph all but chuckled. "Or better yet, try a room with lockable doors."

Sighing in utter relief, Cal tried not to laugh himself. "I'll make sure I'm better prepared next time."

Steph winked. "You do that." Then she tilted her head to the side looking first at Cal's stomach and then at Lucy's waist. Her grin widened and she pointed her right index finger at both of them. "You might want to get cleaned up while Rosie and Mia are still fiddling around with the CDs. I don't think they'll leave you alone if they see those powder marks."

As Cal glanced down at himself, he noticed Lucy do the same. Light, uneven flour handprints were scattered across each of them. Even though he'd been aware of the flour on the breadboard, the dough, and the rolling pin, when his lust for her had taken over, he hadn't given it a second thought. His smile was broad as he looked back up at Lucy, but her wide eyes were filled with mortification.

"Don't worry," he told her, soothingly. "It'll brush off." He reached out to touch her, but she quickly backed away.

"I…I think—" She swallowed quickly and then looked over at Steph. "I'm just going to go to the bathroom to clean up."

Offering her a curious frown, Steph nodded.

With a final glance at Cal, her contorted brows making her expression appear almost apologetic, Lucy turned to head toward the hallway and left the room.

Turning back to Steph, Cal speedily dusted himself free of the white powdery traces of his romantic interlude with Lucy. He caught a glimpse of the twinge of empathy that flickered across Steph's concerned expression, before she spoke again.

"Don't take it to heart, Cal." Her tone seemed filled with sincere understanding. "It's obvious Lucy cares about you. She just needs some time to come to terms with that."

Regretfully, Cal nodded. "I know," he told her. And he did understand, but that didn't stop him from wanting things to move faster. He wanted and needed Lucy now and he knew she felt the same. They had already let enough time pass them by and Cal wasn't about to let her have another fourteen years without him in her life. He couldn't handle it, wouldn't survive it. He would just have to find a way to convince her that they should be together and that fighting their connection, the enduring love they had for each other, was pointless.

***

"Did you really?" Cal looked at Lucy incredulously.

He was seated at the head of Steph and Mia's dining table, adjacent to her, and if he moved his left hand just an inch, it would be covering part of her right. Feeling suddenly too close to him in their cozy corner, Lucy leaned farther back in her chair, removing her hands from the tabletop. She felt her eyebrows knit nervously as she frowned.

"Um, maybe." Her voice was so quiet that she wondered if anyone actually heard her.

Judging by the abundance of empty beer bottles littering the tabletop, Lucy estimated that it had probably been a couple of hours since they'd finished eating dinner. Plates with scraps and crumbs of their tasty meal still sat before them on the long, gun-metal grey dining room table, while the remainder of the fresh food put on the kitchen's island for pizza preparation had been plastic wrapped and placed back in the fridge for another day.

At Mia's suggestion a little while ago, most of the women had removed their shoes in search of further comfort, letting their bare feet stretch and relax against the cool white tiles on the dining room floor. Only Steph and Cal had opted to keep their work shoes in place. Beginning to feel utterly exhausted and preparing herself to face the brunt of Cal's reaction, Lucy tucked her warm feet beneath her on the chair, pulling herself into more of a protective ball. She suspected Rosie was similarly tired as she seemed dangerously close to a giggle-fit. Though that could have been due to the fact that she was very tipsy—or the fact that it had been her idea to bring up this awkward topic of conversation.

Lucy knew Steph and Mia were watching her closely from where they sat together across the table. A few minutes ago, Mia had moved from her seat next to Rosie, to perch lovingly on Steph's lap, hugging her around the neck as she cuddled against her. They had been very quiet since Rosie had shared the intimate detail and Lucy had to wonder if that was their way of helping or if they, too, were very weary. She just hoped they weren't silently laughing at the whole situation.

"Luce?" Cal's tone was eager, prompting her to tell him the truth she knew he wished to know.

Lucy offered him a timid shrug. "I'd always assumed that Maddy had told you."

Cal's blue-grey eyes widened and he let out a scoffing sound in surprise. "That you referred to me as a *bome*? The bane of your existence? Yeah, she would never have told me that." He laughed again, a loud, hearty chortle of a sound.

As Rosie giggled along with him, Lucy couldn't help but feel relieved that Cal was so amused. She'd planned never to tell him, fearing the ensuing shouting that she believed would be bound to follow. Clearly, she'd misjudged him.

"I actually really like the sound of it," he said as he glanced at Steph and Mia with a huge, white grin.

Lucy followed suit, noting the rocking of Mia's shoulders as she struggled not to laugh and the smirk of satisfaction that tugged at the corner of Steph's mouth. Traitors though they were, Lucy was still glad the revelation was a smooth and humorous one. If she had any extra energy—or if she could stop, for just a second, thinking about the passionate kiss Cal and she had shared earlier—then maybe, just maybe she would be able to laugh along as well.

Then Cal's captivating gaze met hers again and his sexy wink was devilish. "It makes us sound like an old, married couple." He leaned forward in his chair, moving himself as close to her as he could without leaving his seated position. "In fact, I like it so much, I'm thinking about giving you a nickname too."

Lucy swallowed nervously—or at least she hoped that unsettling feeling in the bottom of her stomach was nerves. The heat from Cal's strong body seemed to radiate toward her along with the warm, spicy scent of his skin. She was having trouble focusing, her gaze desperate to drop to his full lips. She'd already noticed the dark blond of the five o'clock shadow that graced his firm, square-shaped jaw. Her fingers itched to stroke it, she needed to touch it, to nibble at that perfect honey skin. The tug of sensation near her stomach dug deeper, lower, and Lucy knew she could no longer blame it on nerves. It was pure desire, raw and hungry.

"What's that?" she asked, her voice no more than a squeak of sound.

Cal's expression became even more wicked. "Well, as I'm the quasi-husband in this scenario, I think the most appropriate nickname would be…." He paused, licking his lips as he stared into her eyes. "Wife."

Lucy froze. Was he serious? She felt like slapping him for using a term that his commitment-phobic, womanizing ways completely derided. Could he be that insensitive? Yet, her heart swelled, and she suddenly wanted to kiss him all over again. Did he mean it? Did Cal think of her like that, as wife-material?

Before her thoughts could derail and mentally accuse him of playing a cruel joke once more, the room erupted in laughter. Lucy dragged her stunned gaze from Cal to glance around the table at her so-called friends. Rosie and Steph were chuckling, their bodies rocking with the erupting sound, while Mia's expression was bright, excitement filling her eyes as her Cheshire-cat grin beamed.

Lucy found herself smiling as she looked back at Cal. His wide grin in return softened slightly, lovingly and his expression filled with affection. It had been funny after all, and damn clever, she was able to appreciate that. Just because she was silently fighting the urge to steal him away and lock him in her bedroom for a month in the hope of getting all her dirty desires out of her system, didn't mean that she'd lost her sense of humor. And he'd definitely had every right to tease her, especially after discovering what she'd referred to him as for the last fourteen years. It just bothered her a little bit to know that some part of her had hoped so dearly that he'd meant it, that he could easily think of her as his *wife*.

CHAPTER TWELVE

Lucy knew she should have said no. It had been a dangerous proposal for many reasons, least of all the fact that she and Cal would be attending together.

After dinner at Steph and Mia's flat and after blatantly refusing to let Cal drive her home as he'd offered, she'd agreed to let him walk her to the nearby tram stop. Perhaps that's where her true mistake lay. Had she not allowed them to be alone together—again—then maybe she would have had more strength to refuse him, as she had in front of Steph when he'd asked to take her the few minutes down the road to her townhouse in his chauffeur driven Range Rover. Maybe if she'd been strong, if she'd just thanked him for his consideration and headed into the shadows of the streetlamp-lit street alone, she wouldn't be in the mess she now found herself in.

Why? Why did I say yes?

Lucy knew why. She'd wanted to spend more time with Cal. Although it hadn't really been a surprise. She had so thoroughly enjoyed the time she'd spent with him at work and socializing with her close friends that she desired those good times to continue. Every time they were together, she was reminded of how much she'd missed his company over the past decade and how much she enjoyed talking, joking, and laughing with him. He'd always been her best friend; she could barely remember a time before knowing him. Even when she'd hated him, she'd missed him, loved him. He was in every fiber of her being, so much so that the more time she spent around him, the more she craved to be around him. She'd known she was addicted, known he was her weakness, yet the more time she was with him, the more she gave in to it all.

As soon as Cal had suggested the Sunday luncheon at Rob and Maddy's, Lucy's mind had been screaming at her to decline the offer. "No" was on the tip of her tongue, but her heart had gotten excited, beating out a rapid, rhythmic dance in her chest. It was another chance to be with him and the thought of the three best friends in the one place after all these years had given her a child-like eagerness. She knew she'd probably regret it, but she'd said it anyway—*yes*.

Suddenly, her smartphone vibrated, making a buzzing noise on the small, glass-topped table beside the outdoor chaise lounge she was reclining upon in Rob and Maddy's backyard. As Lucy glanced over at it, reaching instinctively to answer it, an image of Trent appeared on the screen. He had been calling and texting her regularly since their encounter in the photocopy room, but Lucy had done her best to ignore all attempts at communication. Even though she hated to admit it, he had really unnerved her that day, and she didn't feel as though anything she said to him would smooth things over.

Days ago, soon after it happened, Lucy had texted him a message to explain what she hadn't been able to say in the moment. She had put it kindly, that although she had tried in the past to embrace him in a more intimate relationship, unfortunately her feelings for him had never grown further than that of friendship—and that was stretching the truth as it was, but she wouldn't tell him that. The replies she'd received after that were incessant, demanding and ludicrously possessive, so she had decided that keeping her distance and giving him time to simmer down were probably her best options.

Touching the side of the mobile phone, she switched the power off, then grabbed the glass of homemade lemonade beside it and relaxed back into the chair. With her sunglasses shielding both the harsh midday sun and the direction of her gaze, Lucy couldn't help but stare across the paved courtyard in front of her to where Cal was talking to Rob beside the barbecue. The appetizing smell of beef patties and grilling onions wafted over to her as the sizzling sound of them cooking made the men's conversation inaudible. Absent-mindedly, she twirled the green straw in the tall, icy cold glass in her hand.

Did he just propose? Mia's whispered words whirled back to the front of Lucy's mind, lingering there again, haunting her as they had ever since Mia had first spoken them.

She'd stopped Lucy on her way out the door on Friday evening as Cal was saying his goodbyes to Steph and Rosie further inside the flat. A grin of elation brightened her features, her eyes glittering with excitement and surprise when she'd grabbed Lucy's arm and bent closer to her ear.

"Did he just propose?" Those hushed words had made Lucy's heart somersault in her chest.

Surely teasing her with the nickname *wife* and actually proposing were not the same thing. Yet, Mia had thought so or at the very least, she'd thought it had been Cal's way of preparing Lucy for the idea. Lucy had thought her friend was reading signs that weren't there, putting too much belief into something that was certainly no more than Cal's mischievous sense of humor. However, that hadn't stopped her from hoping.

As soon as she realized she'd mentally admitted such an atrocious, almost treacherous interest in the prospect of marriage to Cal—the once bane of her existence—Hawthorne, Lucy nearly choked swallowing her own saliva.

"You right there, hon?" Maddy appeared beside her.

Lucy drank deeply from the chilled drink in her hand and then took a steadying breath. "Fine."

With a hushed giggle, Maddy took a seat on the outdoor chaise lounge chair beside the one Lucy was stretched out in. She filled her own empty glass and then placed the fresh pitcher of lemonade on the small wooden table between them. After taking a drink herself, Maddy relaxed into the chair and crossed one white linen pant-covered leg over another. As she straightened her snug, blue and white striped shirt she glanced over at Lucy, offering her a cheeky grin.

"Do you want to go over and top up the boys' glasses? I think Cal's is empty."

Lucy turned to her best friend, glaring at her from behind the dark, shaded lenses of her elegant sunglasses. "You're enjoying this way too much," she growled.

Maddy pouted. "Give me a break. I haven't had the three of us in the same room for almost fifteen years. I think I deserve a little time to gloat." A wide smile spread her lips again. "Besides, I thought you and Cal were getting along well these days?"

Murmuring a non-committal response, Lucy slumped back into her chair and glanced around at the decorative backyard. Maddy and Rob's house was ten minutes from St. Kilda Beach on a family-friendly, tree-lined avenue and had been built to suit their love for entertaining. Inside, the house was spacious and bright, with lots of large picture windows and comfy seating areas, while outside, the stunning paved courtyard looked as though it had come straight from a *House and Garden* magazine. Well-trimmed hedges and flowering shrubs lined the fence, along with a few other stylish arrangements in giant colorful pots. As well as the two outdoor lounges she and Maddy were currently enjoying, there was also a full outdoor furniture setting to her left with enough chairs to fit eight people and a hand-carved wooden bench seat near the barbecue.

As Lucy's gaze roamed back to the men who were laughing jovially at something she hadn't quite heard over the noise of their lunch cooking, she couldn't help but admire them.

With their background so similar to a magazine spread, both Rob and Cal—very attractive in their own right—appeared even more like posed cover models. They were both casually dressed in denim jeans, yet Cal's pants seemed to accentuate his sexy backside and strong thighs to somewhat illegal standards. Rob's olive-colored, Lacoste collared shirt was fashionably preppy, while Cal's large biceps were set to flex freely beneath his tight, black t-shirt. Like his wife, Rob was wearing designer flip-flops whereas Cal had opted for loafers.

Her hidden gaze continued to rake over Cal as he turned slightly to glance back at her. His sandy blond hair was unusually mussed, making the length of his fringe seem longer and his appearance that bit rougher. His square jaw was coarse with a day or so of dark blond stubble, while his full, cupid's bow lips looked delectably kissable. Lucy watched carefully as his tongue sneaked out to wet them lightly. Feeling her own body tighten in response, nipples hardening as tingles gripped her insides, she nearly groaned out loud. It was totally unfair of her body to want him so much, her lust burning through her like an internal betrayal. She was the one who had told him she needed more time, that she wanted to get to know him, to become friends once more before they took things any further and now all she wanted to do was rip his clothes off. Of course, she still needed time. Didn't she?

Lucy's gaze rose to Cal's black designer sunglasses. Even though they hid the expression in his eyes, the twitch of a smirk that pulled at his lips seemed to be enough to help her guess what he might be thinking.

"Are you planning to talk to me at all during your stay or are you just going to stare at Cal the whole time?"

Grimacing in annoyance at her best friend's remark,

Lucy turned her attention back to Maddy. "Someone's feeling sassy today."

Maddy's grin was sickly sweet. "It's one of the best days of my life, so I'm feeling rather chipper, yeah."

Lucy had to smile at that. "Thanks for putting up with my drama for all these years, Maddy. I know it was a lot to expect."

The features of Maddy's pretty face softened and her expression became sincere. "I may not have agreed with your chosen form of punishment, but I understand why you did it. I know how much he hurt you, Luce."

The compassion in Maddy's voice had Lucy looking away back toward the barbecue. Cal was once again focused on a story Rob was telling.

"I think he's grown up a bit since then."

Out of the corner of her eye, Lucy noticed Maddy's gaze follow hers.

"A bit," Maddy agreed, her tone teasing. A long silence seemed to pass between them before Maddy spoke again. "Have you told him why?"

Lucy shook her head.

"You want him to guess?"

Straightening in her chair, Lucy placed her glass on the table between them and sighed when she noticed Maddy's curious expression. With her right hand, she raised her sunglasses and propped them on the top of her head. She stared at Maddy, willing her to understand. Sure, it may have seemed unreasonable, but if Cal had ever truly been her best friend, if he'd ever really cared about her, known her as well as he'd claimed, then he should've been able to realize the truth, to notice when he'd broken her heart.

"I just want him to know," Lucy told her.

*

Lucy was taunting him. She had to be. Why else would she have worn that dress? Its light, mauve material was snug around her perky, bra-less breasts and then hung loosely down to mid-thigh, revealing those shapely legs Cal longed to have wrapped around him again. The thin spaghetti straps and floral-patterned crochet at the back did little to shield her creamy, touchable skin from the coolness of the nearing evening.

He knew he was staring at her as she walked around the wooden table toward him, but he didn't care. Her attention was focused on Madison.

Lucy laughed. "I'd forgotten all about that." She placed the cheese platter she'd been holding in the middle of the table and took her seat next to him.

With a bottle of red wine in her hand, Madison sat down next to Rob on the other side of the large alfresco dining setting in the corner of the courtyard. "I bet you remember, Cal. After all, you both had to put me to bed twice."

Reluctantly, Cal dragged his gaze from where it lingered on Lucy's beguiling figure. He knew he was losing control again. If his lustful stares weren't enough to prove that to her, then the growing bulge tightening the crotch of his pants would be enough to confirm any suspicions. He forced a look at Madison. Of course, he knew what she was referring to. Toby's parties were fond memories for all of them and this one in particular held some of the best.

"Toby's end of junior year party. His dodgy friend Rouso scored some bottles of vodka from his Russian uncle." Cal paused. "If I remember correctly, you challenged Claire Ivers to a drinking contest. Claire won."

"Hey!" Madison growled at him. "She only won because you guys dragged me away."

"And why did we do that?" The sweetness of Lucy's voice, even with its playful tone, had Cal staring at her again.

Madison frowned innocently. "Because you're party-poopers."

That had Rob laughing loudly.

Lucy cast an amused look Cal's way and liquid fire shot through his veins.

It would be inappropriate to make love to her right here, wouldn't it?

Cal almost rolled his eyes at the ridiculousness of his thought. Of course, it would be. His gaze raked over her pink lips, that delicate bare neck and then down to the tempting peaks of her full breasts, before rising to her face again. He wanted to touch her so badly, his whole body ached for it. Maybe he could slip his hand into hers, wrap an arm around her shoulders or spread his fingers over the smooth skin of her thigh? Maybe that small touch would be enough to quell his hunger for her?

He bit his lower lip in frustration. Who was he kidding? He'd ravage her as soon as he touched her. Cal clenched his itchy fingers into fists instead.

Then, Lucy's gaze left him for Madison again and he felt suddenly cold.

"We would have locked you in that room," Lucy said, "except for the fact that the lock was on the inside."

"I didn't want to miss out on the fun." Madison pouted at her husband as though hoping he might offer her some support.

Cal forced his thoughts away from the searing image of Lucy's nipples pricking in the chilly air beneath the soft fabric of her dress. He gave Madison a grin. "It might have still been early, but you were well past drunk. You were just lucky that Toby offered up his own room for you to sleep it off in. The rest of us had to share the rec room floor." He risked a glance at Lucy.

She blushed at his words.

Cal had hoped she'd remember. That night had been one of his fondest memories for so long. All those many years ago, once the party had quietened down and only a few had stayed awake to brave the last of the alcohol and the coming morning; when there were teenagers snoring, crammed on top of one another on the couch and strewn over the few beanbags on the carpeted floor, and Toby had reluctantly decided to sleep top and tail in his bed to watch over Madison—Cal and Lucy had snuggled beneath a throw rug in their private little corner.

Cal was supposed to have been dating Jackie Gardener at the time, a petite blonde with red freckles and a wicked temper. When Cal hadn't wanted to leave the party at the unreasonably early time she had, Jackie had thrown a tantrum and left with a couple of girlfriends instead. Lucy had argued hotly with him over his decision, but he'd quickly told her that he hadn't wanted to leave Madison in her drunk state—never mind the fact that he had no plans at all to leave Lucy alone herself either. Once everyone had settled down to sleep, she'd blatantly refused to lie down close beside him, purposely keeping her distance. But, as soon as she'd started shivering, he was there, covering her with the warmth of his body, holding her close, his firm body against the soft line of hers as he nuzzled her neck and breathed in the sweet, honey scent of her—and she hadn't pushed him away. It had been heaven and he'd never wanted to let her go.

As he reflected, Cal felt a gratified grin spread his lips and then, in seeing Madison's confusion, immediately regretted it.

"Okay, what did I miss?" Madison was watching him carefully, as though she was trying to decipher a secret code.

Cal shook his head and offered her the most innocent expression he could muster. "Nothing. I was just remembering how much fun we had."

Madison frowned. "That's not what that look was." Then, she glanced at Lucy and Cal followed her gaze.

Her face still rosy with a heated blush, Lucy wouldn't look either of them in the eye. Instead, she stared down into the stained depths of her empty wine glass.

Madison's hazel eyes returned to his and narrowed suspiciously. "What aren't you telling me?"

As though recognizing the rising hostility in the room, Rob leaned forward and grabbed Madison's hand, caressing her palm with his fingers. "Maybe it's better if we don't know," he told her, his voice jovial, but firm.

Cal's gaze flicked to Rob, but he wasn't brave enough to make any sort of grateful gesture to the man, lest Madison read too far into that as well. Hardening his gaze, Cal stared Madison down. "You going to pour that Shiraz or is there a corkage fee?"

After a brief stint at a death-staring contest, Madison rolled her eyes at him and then relaxed into her chair. "You know I'll get it out of you eventually," she told him, her tone almost smug. "In fact, this bottle of wine might get me that bit closer to the truth."

Cal acknowledged the challenge with a haughty chuckle. "Good luck with that."

Shaking his head with a smile, Rob grabbed the bottle of red wine from Madison's firm grasp and set about unscrewing the cap. "Now, now, children," he chided them carefully. "Let's play nice while we're still in friendly company." Rob nodded toward Lucy.

As Cal and Madison glanced toward her, Lucy stood abruptly.

"I should probably be going." Her face was still flushed as she struggled to hold Rob's surprised gaze.

A sharp shock of dread sparked through Cal's nerves at her words.

"No—" Rob and Madison began in unison. They shared a quick look and then Madison let Rob continue, even though it was obvious she was desperate to speak.

"There's no need to leave, Lucy. It's still early and," he glanced at Madison again before continuing, "we'd be happy for you to stay for dinner as well. It's no trouble, really."

"Please, Luce." Madison's eyes were wide, her expression forlorn.

Wringing her hands together as she nibbled at her

lower lip, Lucy cast a wary look across at Cal.

He smiled up at her, doing his best to appear non-threatening and friendly, not desperate or lustful, and definitely not as though he longed to throw her down on the table and ravish her in front of their friends.

Rob grabbed Lucy's empty wine glass and started pouring the Shiraz. "Really, Lucy. It's fine." His kind expression and gentle words oozed reassurance. "We're changing the subject, anyway." He glanced purposefully at Madison. "Aren't we, Mads?"

Still staring at Lucy, Madison nodded obediently. "Yes. Definitely. What would you like to talk about, Luce?"

Lucy grimaced and then looked helplessly toward the house as though seeking out an exit.

Rob reached out toward her with the refreshed glass of wine in his hand, offering it to her. "Come on. Give it a little longer and if you still feel like heading home after that, we'll even pay for your cab fare."

After a minute, which felt like a century to Cal, Lucy released a tremendous sigh and stopped wringing her hands. She shrugged anxiously and eventually took her seat again.

"Sorry," she told them, her beautiful blue eyes focused on Rob.

Smiling, he moved the glass closer to her, and she took it from him. "It's all good." His tone was soft and compassionate as he grabbed Madison's hand and held it lovingly in his. "It's been an overwhelming day for all of us." He gazed briefly at Madison before looking back at Lucy. "We've had lots of catching up to do and, hopefully, in the future we'll have plenty more opportunities to do the same."

Madison's hopeful grin was incandescent.

Cal knew how she felt. The day had been amazing, as had every other moment he'd managed to spend with Lucy, but today was even more special than usual. Today, three best friends had finally been reunited in laughter, harmony, and love. It was like old times again and Cal couldn't imagine his future without it.

***

Cal had actually asked his chauffeur, Henry, to step outside—out of the Range Rover the older man was supposed to be in charge of driving. The situation made Lucy feel even more apprehensive than when she'd first stepped into the confined space of the sport utility vehicle with him.

"I hope you don't mind, but I needed us to be alone." Cal's tone was calming and sincere, but neither did very much to help settle Lucy's nerves.

She nodded toward him, but maintained her distance. Since sitting inside on the black leather interior, she'd scooted as far away from him and as close to the adjacent door as she could. Lucy needed to be able to make a quick escape if necessary, for she had been certain if Cal didn't attempt to make a move on her during their travel time, then she was at the risk of doing so herself.

The dark backstreet outside appeared quiet in the stillness of Sunday night. It had been nearing ten o'clock when they'd left Maddy and Rob's house and that, if she judged the distance correctly, had been about half an hour ago. Lucy was almost home. They were on her street, so close to her townhouse that she could've sworn she could see the burgundy color of her front door. Yet, Cal had asked Henry to pull over to the curb just far enough away that for her to jump out and run for safety would be an awkwardly obvious statement.

Lucy dragged her gaze away from the darkness outside the car and tried to hold Cal's blue-grey gaze. "It was a lot of fun today," she told him, when he didn't make a move to explain their seclusion.

Cal smiled, his full lips not quite parting. It would have been a warm, affectionate expression had his eyes not glittered with a lustful hunger.

After attempting to swallow her jittery nerves, Lucy forced her features to brighten. She was sure she must have looked like some kind of trapped animal, desperately searching for escape, but she was a big girl, not a timid teenager and there was no sensible reason for her fear. She was a grown woman and she could control her own inappropriate desires.

Even as she repeated the mantra in her head, it didn't seem to help calm her. In fact, her impish imagination was doing its best to focus on one thing in particular—*her desires*. Quiet, kind, salt-and-pepper-haired Henry may have been only right outside the car, but that didn't stop Lucy fantasizing about having Cal screw her brains out right then and there.

"Luce...," Cal began slowly, making Lucy even more anxious.

Beginning to babble, she cut him off. "I-it was funny when Maddy found out you knew about the *bome* thing." She laughed and it sounded too sharp, too loud to her own ears, that she quickly stopped. "I thought she was going to kill me," she tittered.

Cal's gaze narrowed in concern and he reached out to her, seeking her hand with his.

Without thinking, Lucy jolted away from him and harder against the car door. She knew her eyes were wide; her expression was fearful and she was suddenly mortified by her reaction.

"I'm so sorry," she told him quickly, her head lowering.

After an instant, Lucy braved a look up at him, but instead of seeing the frustration of harsh rejection or anger of misunderstanding she expected to see, Cal was just staring at her, his expression peaceful, his eyes determined.

"Luce," he began again, his voice caressing her like velvet.

Clenching her jaw, she fought the urge to interrupt, to turn the conversation back to lighter topics. This time she would hear him out, she owed him that after acting like such a childish scaredy-cat.

His kissable lips parted into a smile. "You have to stop fighting this, baby." He reached out and stroked a loose strand of hair behind her ear.

The sensation was electrifying and sent shivers throughout her whole body. Her nipples tightened, hoping and anticipating their own turn, while hot desire pooled at the delta of her thighs. As he cupped her face with his hand, she fought the need to rub her cheek against him, to attack his coarse palm with her lips. Breathing deeply, Lucy tried to calm the burning need clutching at her heart, making it race.

"I know you wanted to take things slow," he told her carefully, "but there's something special between us. You and I both know that, we've always known it." His thumb caressed her cheek lightly. "You need to give it a chance. Give us a chance, Luce. What is there to be afraid of?"

She stared at him. He had to be joking. There were plenty of reasons for her to be afraid—the main one being the fear of losing her best friend, the man she had always loved all over again and suffering from a final, irreparably broken heart.

Lucy opened her mouth, but no words formed. Every cell in her being wanted to give in to what Cal was offering, give in to what her heart and libido longed for, but realistically she knew there was a chance that it wouldn't end well.

"Please give this a chance, Luce," Cal repeated. He leaned closer to her, his brows furrowed and his gaze desperate.

Gnawing on her bottom lip, she felt her heart leap in her chest as though bouncing in agreement. Was it really that easy? Could she just give in—to him, to everything? Could she just ignore the danger of the relationship failing all over again? Was it possible to just forgive him for all the hurt he caused her and move forward? Lucy just didn't know, but suddenly all she wanted to do was try.

Ignoring the uneasiness in her gut, that last shred of sense questioning the risk to her emotional wellbeing, Lucy did what she'd been longing to do—she turned her head and kissed his palm. When her gaze found Cal's again, she was languidly relishing the feel of his warm hand against her soft cheek. His smoky-blue eyes darkened sensually as he watched her. His strong, broad body poised just in front of her, like a panther having sighted its prey.

Lucy sighed, partly in exhaustion, elation, and satisfaction. "Okay," she told him, her voice breathy. "What would I need to do?"

Cal's gaze dropped to her lips.

Her breath caught in her throat, anticipation locking her in place as her body thrummed, longing to be touched.

"Well," Cal pondered, licking his lips as he spoke. "I think you should come to the Gold Coast with me."

CHAPTER THIRTEEN

Although Cal had hoped that all the contractors would be off the site before he and Lucy arrived at the Calypso on the morning of Tuesday the twenty-first of April, he had been realistic. After all, he had been expecting a great deal from them, cramming at least two months of work into just over a fortnight.

He'd noted the lone painter's pickup truck as the black limousine he'd hired entered the driveway of the fourteen-story hotel off Main Beach Parade, the major street along the parallel coastline. While he couldn't see the owners of the vehicle, he hoped they were inside finishing up the last of their tasks, so that there wouldn't be any issues with the placement of internal or external furnishings. After today, they had one final day as a grace period before the public would arrive and inundate the rejuvenated building.

As instructed, the chauffeur parked the luxury car just outside the shaded awning of the hotel's grand porte-cochere. Once Cal had exited the limo, he held the door open for Lucy to do the same and then they both stepped back to admire the striking view before them.

The entire facade of the Calypso had been modernized. It's once colorfully bright paint job had been replaced with a clean, classy ivory complemented by royal blue accentuating necessary design lines. The previously shabby sign on top of the elegant porte-cochere had been completely redesigned in the new colors the Insight Marketing team had chosen to match the Calypso's fresh family-friendly persona and was outlined with neon tube lighting. The crisp whites, ocean blues and sparse beach yellows gave the complex a fashionable, inviting feel. Cal was certain, once lit up for the evening, the development would look just as impressive in the night.

"Wow." Lucy's gasp of admiration mirrored his own feelings perfectly.

Glancing in her direction, he grasped onto her hand as the limo's chauffeur retrieved their luggage from the trunk. "A little different from the last time you were here, isn't it?"

She nodded, but didn't take her gaze from the impressiveness of the Calypso's welcoming entry.

"Come on, let's—" Cal began, before noticing Paul dash out of the sliding glass doors at the entrance and hurry toward them.

Although his large blue eyes and thick head of dark, possibly dyed, hair gave him a youthful appearance, Cal knew the older man was nearing sixty. He was positively beaming, his smile nearly splitting his face, as he rushed over to greet them in his pristine black suit, white business shirt and royal blue tie. Seeing the elation in Paul's eyes, Cal found himself grinning like an excited child again. The man was almost kin to both him and Lucy. He had witnessed them grow up and had regularly been present for some of the most enjoyable times in both their lives. Until now, thinking of how many years it had been since he'd last seen Paul in person, Cal hadn't realized just how much he'd missed his quasi-uncle.

"Mr. Gillies?" Lucy posed the surprised greeting as a question.

Slowing as he neared her, Paul opened his arms and

dragged Lucy into a tight hug. "Little Lucy," he sighed nostalgically. "When did you get so tall?"

Lucy laughed. "I'm sure it's just the high heels."

Chuckling, Paul released her, but kept his hands on her shoulders. "It's so good to see you." He glanced at Cal, his affectionate grin tugging at Cal's heartstrings. "Both of you. It's been too long."

He enveloped Lucy into a second cuddle, before releasing her again and wrapping his arms around Cal for a brief, but very warm, masculine embrace. As the two men let go of each other and stepped back, Cal noticed the light glistening of unshed tears in the hotel manager's eyes.

"It's Paul now," Paul said, glancing at Lucy. "No more *Mr. Gillies, can I please have an ice-cream?* Or *Mr. Gillies, can we please use the inflatable tires for the pool?* It's just Paul, okay?"

Lucy giggled and then reached out to rub Paul's upper arm tenderly. "Of course, *Paul*," she agreed. "We're family after all."

Appearing very pleased with that announcement, Paul nodded and then took Lucy's hand, before linking her arm in the crook of his. He gently patted the back of her hand as his expression filled with excitement. "I can't wait to show you what a wonderful job the contractors have done inside. You're both going to love it!"

As Paul led Lucy toward the Calypso's entrance, Cal followed close behind them, a stupidly happy smile still spreading his lips. His heart hadn't felt so full, his chest so light, in such a long time. His plans for the Calypso were travelling well, his efforts to save the beloved building were actually paying off, and the love of his life was about to spend the next few days enjoying the coastal lifestyle of the sunny Gold Coast with him. It seemed as though life was finally starting to go his way.

***

Arms wide in a starfish style, Lucy let herself fall

backward into the cloud-like embrace of the brand-new bed. She had just left Cal in the hallway, promising to meet him outside their rooms in an hour to continue on to dinner. The day had been a lengthy one, but it had been a wonderful experience overall.

It may have taken hours, but Paul had finally finished showing them the extent of the improvements that had been made to the Calypso. Besides the stunning changes to the outside of the building and the enticing facade, the whole inside of the establishment had been painted, cleaned, and decorated to match the newly chosen crisp beach theme.

To Lucy's delight, there was no longer a bar lounge adjacent to the spacious reception desk, which was set to receive a collection of plush, midnight blue sofas in the morning. Instead, the bar had been completely removed and a big game room with pale blue walls had been created. She'd become even more excited once she'd seen that the space was already decked out with numerous modern arcade games, a regular red slate pool table, an air hockey table, and a foosball table. It looked like the average kid's dream playroom and suited the big kid in her just fine. If she was lucky, maybe she'd be able to challenge Cal to a game of car racing on the driving machine during their stay.

Once all three of them had moved into the Great Hall where so many of Toby's interesting childhood plays had debuted, Lucy appreciated just how much had been achieved with its revamp. The Insight Marketing team had spent a great deal of time heavily promoting the unappreciated area as a suitable space for extravagant weddings and business seminars alike and had managed to create a huge public interest. Walking inside, Lucy could see the fruition of their vision. Where she clearly remembered short, narrow maroon drapes hanging in front of the tall windows that overlooked the flower garden outside, she now saw spectacular silk, iceberg white curtains cascading to the floor. Even the carpet of the sizeable function area had changed and become uniform with the rest of the new design, blossoming from a dark red and dull gold pattern to blue and silver hues. Touched by the magnificence of the room, Lucy looked forward to seeing the Great Hall in its element once again with its brand-new tables and chairs full of cheerful guests.

After wandering through the hotel, noting that the majority of the internal and external furnishings had been added and finalized, Paul had proudly offered to escort them around the rest of the hotel's grounds to show them the extent of the landscaping that had been completed the day earlier. As they'd exited the building, the painter and his young female apprentice, who had been finishing the last of the painting in the back-of-house staff area, had waved to them on their own way out. Appearing relieved, Cal had grabbed an affectionate hold of Lucy's hand again and had continued to follow Paul outside. It was as they stepped out into the warm sunlight that the child in Lucy's heart fell in love with the Calypso's pool all over again.

It had been the last of the more extravagant changes and it had been completely redesigned. The kidney-shaped in-ground pool was at the beach-side of the complex and had always been relatively ordinary—but that description no longer applied. At one end, a large circular area had been added to incorporate a spa, while at the other, a huge section of the lawn had been dug out to lengthen it into a tropical, free form shape. As Paul had mentioned to them previously, landscaping around the entire pool had already been laid, including a small, rocky waterfall in the far corner and an arrangement of short palm trees, Hawaiian hibiscus shrubs, and giant, spiky green agaves lining the tiled edge.

Paul had been quick to lead them closer, across the stylish grey and teak sandstone tiles that surrounded the pool and the courtyard area. As they'd gazed down at the empty inner section, he'd explained that it had been set with a cement and quartz mixture called Quartzon, which had created a strong finish to the design and which would sparkle beneath the water in the sunlight. Although it was yet to be filled, with that task having already been organized for tomorrow, the Calypso's contemporary-looking pool appeared to Lucy to be an idyllic, tropical escape for any happy family, fun-loving child, or affectionate couple. Excited by the opportunity of a late-night swim, she'd mentally added it to her list of things to talk Cal into while she was there.

When their excursion of the complex finally came to an end, it seemed obvious to both her and Cal that things were on track for the grand re-opening. There were only a few items, including the outdoor furniture, the reception's sofa set, a second batch of new bed linen, and the embroidered bath and beach towels, that remained and all were supposed to be delivered and arranged the next day. Lucy just couldn't believe how much her once beloved holiday resort had transformed in the last few weeks. All their hard work and long hours and that of all the diligent contractors, had paid off and created the wonderfully, picturesque creation that was the Calypso.

Still reclining on the hotel bed, her eyes closed as her mind raced over the events of the day, Lucy sighed contentedly. It felt incredible to be back in one of her favorite places in the world and to be sharing the experience with the man she loved—even if she wasn't quite ready to admit that to him yet.

Even though Cal had done his best to convince her, less than forty-eight hours ago, to give their blossoming romantic relationship a chance, neither of them had pushed the boundaries to take things to the next level. Whether it was out of fear—for her especially—or because Cal didn't want to pressure her, Lucy was especially grateful for the time they'd had to relax into their new relationship. It had given her a chance to accept her feelings for him and time for their physical mannerisms to develop organically into something comforting and loving, rather than purely lustful.

Her turquoise-blue eyes snapped open at the thought. She couldn't deny that, more often than not, her thoughts of Cal were full of desire and longing. Touching him, even when her hand sat snug in his, was enough to send delicious tingling sensations throughout her body. She ached for him to make love to her, to touch her deeply, intimately and they had come very close a couple of times. Yet, Lucy was still thankful that they hadn't yet taken that final step. Although she was already aware of just how dearly she loved him and that her naïve heart had welcomed him back with open veins, she was still terrified of how much that love would overwhelm her, would consume her once they'd slept together. If he didn't already possess all of her now, her mind, heart, body, and soul, then he definitely would once she'd felt him at home inside her. The thought almost petrified her. She had never loved anyone that much, but knew deep in her very being, that Cal was the one. The one who could give her everything she'd ever wanted and needed, the one who could love her as whole-heartedly and unconditionally as she would love him. Or the one who could destroy her, who could use her, take everything from her, who could break her heart into irreparable pieces and leave her to live alone, empty and despairing.

Even though Lucy had tried, she could never forget the pain he'd inflicted upon her all those years ago. He had broken her heart so deeply that, for a time, she'd actually thought that she'd never be able to love again. But she'd been wrong. She'd always loved Cal; she'd never stopped loving him. Yet, still she wanted him to understand what had happened, needed him to know what he'd done to hurt her so severely that she would want to hide from him, to stay away from him for fourteen long years. It still seemed to elude him and so she avoided bringing it up. She wanted to give him another chance, she really did, but everything, all of it, her love for him, the love he said he had for her, none of it would be enough without that final piece of the puzzle. Lucy needed him to understand the agony that had consumed her back then, so that he would never ever hurt her in that way again.

Another sigh rattled free of her lips, this time full of fear, desperation, and hope. Her chest felt tight and her eyes had widened. As the feelings overcame her again, Lucy sat up, making the firm mattress bounce beneath her with the rapid movement. She took a few steadying breaths and then forced her stiff limbs to relax.

She had to give Cal a chance, had to give the obvious chemistry they had together an opportunity to bloom. He was the one for her, her other half—she knew it, he knew it, and her heart would not let her forget it. As Cal had told her, there was no point in fighting it any longer. It seemed that her destiny had finally caught up to her—and her fourteen years of freedom, of fighting against her fate, had reached their conclusion. Fear or no fear, she owed it to herself to take this leap.

Having calmed herself and become resignedly determined, Lucy reached for the black handbag that had been brought up and left beside the bed with the rest of her luggage. Grabbing her mobile phone, she pressed the power button at the bottom to ignite the screen. Seventeen missed calls and five text messages greeted her. All appeared to be from Trent. Not wanting to deal with the jealous, supercilious, and domineering subject matter that was sure to be in all of them, Lucy resorted to the only thing she thought suitable. With a few, quick taps to the screen, she blocked his number. Whatever Trent needed to share with her that was work related, he could pass through Steph or Julia, otherwise he could keep his personal opinions, accusations, and desires to himself.

After placing her phone on the royal blue bedspread beside her open handbag, Lucy stood up and lifted her purple travel suitcase off the floor and laid it on the mattress. She undid the zip around the bag's edge and then flipped open the top to look inside at its contents. Gazing down at the neatly packed clothes, underwear and toiletry bags, Lucy gnawed at her lower lip.

Where had Cal said they were going to eat again?

Did she dress up, dress down, or cover up? Although her acutely active libido would be begging for her to jump his bones as soon as she saw him, Lucy was pretty sure that tonight, both of them were too tired, if not completely wrecked by the extent of the day's events, to enjoy that experience. After all, when it did happen, it would be their first time together, and that, to Lucy, meant it needed to be special.

***

"Are you freakin' serious?" Steph's voice shrieked out of the smartphone's speaker. "How come I wasn't invited? I'd totally put my hand up to date Cal if it meant I got to go to Dreamworld."

"Um, excuse me." The unimpressed tones of Mia's voice piped up in the background of the call. "First of all, you've already got me remember? Your girlfriend? And secondly, if anyone is being invited to Dreamworld it's me."

Lucy laughed. "Maybe next time. After today, I think I've had my fill of junk food and theme park rides for a while." The groans that answered her on the other end of the line were enough to have her burst into laughter once more. "Okay. Okay. Maybe we have to make a long weekend of it one day?"

There was a loud cheer, most likely from Steph, before Mia spoke again.

"Put her on loudspeaker."

After a short beep, everything on Steph and Mia's end of the line began to sound louder.

"Luce, hon, how're you going?" Mia's tone had become

sweet and sincere.

Lucy smiled, feeling comforted and appreciative of her friend's concern. She knew that both Steph and Mia had been apprehensive about her trip to the Gold Coast with Cal. While they had wanted her to get to know him better and give him an opportunity to show her his true colors and how much he'd matured, they were still aware of how much he was capable of hurting her. Lucy knew that it had been difficult enough for them to hold back their protective instincts when she and Cal had been just down the road from them. But now, only two states away, she was sure it must have been harder. Although they did have their differences at times, they had become as important to her as Maddy, as close to her as sisters. She loved them and would always be grateful to have them watching out for her.

"All good," Lucy told them, making sure they could hear the certainty in her tone. "I've loved seeing the Calypso being reborn. It looks amazing and has already been booked out for the next few months. Cal and Paul are ecstatic. I think they'll reach Cal's target, no trouble."

There was a squeal and Steph chuckled.

"As you can probably tell," Steph said almost matter-of-factly, "Mia is very happy to hear that news."

"We are so staying there when all this is over," Mia told them excitedly. "Girls' weekend. Dreamworld weekend!"

Lucy giggled. "Sounds like a plan, Mia." Then she paused and thought about the question that had been bothering her for the last few days. "So, is everything okay back there? Has anything happened with Trent?"

"Not real—" Steph began, but Mia cut her off.

"He's just being an asshole as usual."

Lucy swallowed. "But, he's okay? He hasn't been too upset?"

Mia scoffed and Steph spoke over her.

"He's fine. A bit grumpy, but otherwise he seems himself. He acted like a tool, Luce, don't feel bad about cutting him off. I've already tried to explain things to him myself, but he wants none of it. I guess it'll just take some time for him to come to terms with the fact that it's not going to happen between the two of you."

"Thanks," Lucy said, nodding in response to Steph's explanation and as a way of reassuring herself. "I guess I'm just dreading having to face him when I get back to work."

"Don't worry, babe," Mia chirped. "We've got your back."

Lucy smiled at the amusing, but kind sentiment.

"Anyway, enough Trent, more Cal. What have the two of you been up to while you've been away? Anything naughty happen that you feel desperate to get off your chest?"

"Mia," Steph scolded her girlfriend.

"What?" Mia's tone was all sweetness and innocence. "I'm allowed to ask."

"Sorry, Luce." Steph's apology was almost a grumble.

Chuckling again, Lucy answered appropriately. "Well, yesterday we went on a day trip to the Currumbin Wildlife Sanctuary and then to Mount Tamborine for the afternoon. It was a tour through one of the companies we'd organized to be affiliated with the Calypso so that our clients would get great discounted deals, especially for families. Cal and I had a lot of fun. He got attacked by Lorikeets during one of the bird feeding sessions at the wildlife park and I got a bit freaked out because of the height of the Tamborine Rainforest Skywalk."

Laughter filled the line before Steph answered.

"That's great, Lucy-cakes." Steph sounded very pleased with Lucy's safe response. "And I'm thrilled that the arrangement Insight Marketing made with Coastal Tours and the like on behalf of the Calypso has worked out so well. Hopefully that will be yet another way to entice customers."

"*Hopefully that will be yet another way to entice customers,*" Mia said in a fast, high-pitched tone as she mimicked her partner. "We get it, Lucy, the Gold Coast is super fun. Now, get to the juicy stuff—has Cal proposed?"

"Ugh," Steph grunted in disappointment. "Mia, babe, cool it. It's early days."

Lucy fought back another laugh. "If he had, Mia," she told her decisively, "I would have started the phone call with that news."

***

Cal was lying in bed in his private room at the Calypso, alone—again. Four nights had passed since he and Lucy had arrived at the hotel and six had passed since he'd convinced her to give their romantic relationship a shot. It had been killing him to wait, to keep his desire for her under control, but he'd had to. He'd needed to be on his game when they'd first arrived, to be prepared for anything and everything that could have happened leading up to the Calypso's re-opening. It was important for him to stay on task, not just for the complex and all its wonderful, loyal staff, but for the fond memories it held of his childhood and for his father's legacy. He'd had to be certain that everything moved smoothly and as planned so that they could be sure to make the same weekly profit as Hawthorne Incorporated's famous resort in Sydney.

But, it was now after ten on Saturday night and he and the Calypso had survived three whole days of being inundated with new—and old—cheerful clients who were more than delighted to see the changes and improvements that had been made. So far, the grand re-opening had been a success. Even though he hadn't yet done the sums or fully discussed the issue with Paul, Cal was almost certain that they had already exceeded the amount he'd needed to produce to secure the property within Hawthorne Incorporated's portfolio. Although he didn't want to jinx anything, he was beginning to feel more at ease with what had been achieved and was starting to trust that everything would succeed as he'd hoped.

With that weight lightening, Cal's thoughts had turned back to Lucy and his yearning to show her just how much he needed her in his life. It had been an incredible couple of weeks. Cal hadn't realized just how marvelous things could be without the constant shadow of secrets around them. Now that Lucy was no longer hiding from him, now that they could visit Madison and Rob, even Toby, together without their friends and family members feeling obliged to keep things from each of them, their lives had become that much simpler.

Of course, there was still one thing that grated on him, one thing that he still couldn't figure out, one secret Lucy still would not spill—how he had hurt her all those many years before. It bothered him more than he wanted to admit to himself that he still couldn't work out what he'd done to injure her so deeply.

Fourteen years ago, he'd been consumed with thoughts of her, he'd wanted her to be his, wanted them to date, to make love, to be together forever. But, he'd been terrified that she'd reject him, that she'd say no, that he'd lose, not only the love of his life, but also his best friend. At that time, in his ignorant youth, he just hadn't been brave enough to take that risk. Instead, he'd been weak and had tried to hide his feelings for her in the empty relationships he'd developed with her friends. He wanted her to see that he was happy, to conceal any hint of romantic feeling toward her so that he didn't scare her away, so she didn't leave him. But that had done the complete opposite and she had still left him, anyway.

Tearing his thoughts away from the painful memory, Cal focused back on their progress, on the new romantic relationship that they were building together. They had both slotted so neatly back into their natural affection for each other, their innate chemistry, a more normal way of life, that Cal couldn't understand how they'd managed before—or how he could ever endure something so horrifically agonizing again. Now that Lucy was back in his life, Cal intended to keep her there and he would do whatever was necessary to ensure that they remained together forever.

In the dark room, Cal stretched an arm above the covers and over to the far side, the empty side of the bed. He caressed the soft cotton, silently wishing Lucy would materialize beneath his fingertips. Sighing disappointedly, Cal moved his arm back and interlocked his fingers over the muscles of his naked chest. He stared at the ceiling, his thoughts drifting back to the blissful moments he had already spent in Lucy's embrace.

Tomorrow, he thought to himself.

Tomorrow would be different. Tomorrow, he would focus all his attention on Lucy and do his best to win her whole heart—and, at the very same time, he would bare all of his to her.

CHAPTER FOURTEEN

"Callum!" A distant male voice blurred insignificantly into the background.

Both Lucy and Cal were so engrossed with each other, with their long-held sensual gazes, their enthralling intimate touches, and their whispered sweet nothings, that neither one of them seemed to notice Paul calling out to them from behind the reception desk as they entered the building.

At Cal's suggestion, they had spent the morning down on the beach. He'd arranged a special picnic for them, full of fresh fruit, croissants, coffee, and freshly squeezed orange juice. Between the time they'd spent eating and drinking, lounging, and snuggling on the wide tartan blanket, they'd also frolicked in the calm surf of the early morning and had attempted to create a sandcastle.

It had been magic, a mixture of breathtaking romance and a poignant recreation of childhood memories. Lucy was in love—in love with the Gold Coast, in love with the Calypso, in love with Cal. She was beginning to acknowledge her feelings for him more and more, and even though she was yet to say them out loud, she had come scarily close to letting those three important words leave her lips on a couple of occasions. Yet, she did love him, so deeply, so passionately, so eternally. Lucy was certain she'd always loved him, even when they were innocent children, even when he'd ripped her heart out when they were teenagers. It was as though they'd been made for each other, they always had been, and fighting it had gotten her nowhere, except straight back into his arms all over again.

"Cal!" The male voice grew louder, more familiar. "Lucy?"

Finally, the piercing noise seemed to register in Lucy's ears. She paused just before they reached the elevator with Cal halting his stride next to her.

"Cal!" There were thumping footsteps now, hurrying toward them across the smooth polished floor of the hotel's lobby.

As though suddenly hearing the voice himself, Cal's loving expression hardened slightly as his eyebrows narrowed in curiosity. Together, he and Lucy looked back toward the entry.

Paul had almost reached them and began to slow his pace when he saw them glance back. "Didn't you hear me?" He posed the question to Cal, but an enormous smile overrode the slight puzzlement in his tone.

Appearing a little embarrassed, Cal shook his head. "No. Sorry, Paul," he said as he moved toward the older man, greeting him politely with a light touch to his shoulder. "I was distracted. Is everything okay?"

"Is everything okay?" Paul repeated, his eyes widened as though Cal's question was absurd in some way. He clasped his hands together in a prayer-like position and then released them again. "More than okay, Callum. More than okay."

Lucy frowned, glancing between them as she tried to figure out what had happened.

Cal's smile never reached his eyes when he replied. "That's good." Then he paused as though waiting, hoping that Paul might offer a further explanation.

Paul laughed and threw his hands in the air, looking elated and exasperated at the same time. "Sorry, I just don't know where to start," he spat out between chuckles. "Cal," Paul said as he took Cal's hand in his. "Lucy." He moved to grab her hand as well. "We've done it!" It was almost a yell. "We've gone above and beyond our expected profit. The Calypso is saved!"

Striding forward, he let go of their hands and wrapped his arms around them both, pulling them into an awkward joint embrace.

"Are you serious?" Lucy knew her tone sounded incredulous, but she really needed to hear it from him again.

Paul hugged them closer and then freed them. With a step back, he turned to look at her, his big, blue eyes glowing with excitement. "Yes, honey. I've just finished doing the calculations. This week alone, we've made almost twice the amount that Cal had hoped for. It's all thanks to the renovations, the marketing, and the commission from the tour deals."

His white grin was stretched wide across his face as he glanced away from her and back to Cal. "When you first told me what you wanted to achieve, I wasn't sure it was possible. Yet, we did it! All your ideas, all your plans came together to give the Calypso a second lease on life. It just proves that the Calypso will always be a paradise for families."

Cal's attractive features were lit up with glee as he looked over at Lucy. "I'd thought...," he began, before pausing as though thinking over his words. "I'd *hoped* that we'd reached our target, but still, I just can't believe it."

His expression softened with a look of relief and then he grabbed her in his arms, lifting her feet from the ground and then spinning her around. The happy sound that escaped his lips could have been called a squeal had it not still held a husky, masculine edge.

Lucy heard laughter erupt from Paul, who had backed away a few steps in order to let Cal enjoy the moment to the fullest, and found herself giggling uncontrollably.

They had actually done it! They'd saved the Calypso from sale!

She let out an excited yip and hugged Cal closer before burying her face against the warm, spicy flesh of his neck. He spun her around again, his strong hands dangerously close to the top of her turquoise bikini briefs beneath the white cotton of her long, loose shirt. The feeling of his fingers though the thin material, grasping onto such sensitive skin was enough to make her grateful that he was still dressed in his blue button-down shirt, long black and navy board-shorts, and beige loafers. Had he been shirtless as he had been earlier with her down on the golden sand of the beach, she may not have been able to control herself in public.

Gently, Cal lowered her sandal-covered feet to the floor and then cupped a hand over her cheek. His salty lips covered hers before she had a chance to think. The kiss was invigorating and loving and tasted of the surf and the sweetness of the honey that he'd had on his croissant. His velvet tongue probed into the depths of her mouth needing attention and acceptance, melting her insides, and boiling her blood. Her desperate need built until she'd nearly decided that the lobby, in front of Paul and all the incoming and outgoing guests, was as good a place as any to make love to Cal.

Then their kiss ended abruptly and Cal stepped away, but kept one hand still clasping hers. He grinned at Paul, whose expression had warmed with affection upon seeing their amorous display.

"I can't wait to tell Jack," Cal told him. "Do you have the information handy?"

Paul nodded and then hurried back to the reception desk.

Leading Lucy along with him, Cal followed close behind. Paul ducked around the counter, searching on the staff side of the desk before raising a handful of papers. With a look of triumph, he exited the space and handed the information to Cal.

"The sheets below contain all the bookings we've received since we've reopened, including those placed in anticipation of the re-opening. The piece of paper on top is the tallied income and net-profit for our first week of service with the values of all the current and future bookings totaled at the bottom."

As Paul explained, Cal gazed at the data in front of him, shuffling through the pages, one by one, to better analyze what he was looking at.

"If you need anything further," Paul continued, "There's a few more statistics I haven't yet printed out, graphs, etcetera, showing the growth in sales and the extrapolated income for the next six months."

Cal nodded and gave the hotel manager an appreciative smile. "Thanks, Paul. This is fabulous." Then he glanced down at Lucy. "Do you mind? I'll just be a moment. I need to tell Jack the good news."

Chuckling, Lucy grinned up at him. "Of course. Go ahead. I can meet you back down here in an hour."

His excited expression in return reminded her of the kind-hearted little boy she used to know.

"Thank you," he told her and then he showed her how grateful he was with a brief, soft kiss to her lips.

After sharing his beaming grin with Paul once more, Cal hastened to the privacy of the hotel's back office, beyond the reception desk. When he'd disappeared, Lucy turned around and began to walk back to the internal elevators.

"And where are you off to?" Paul's cheerful voice stopped her.

She spun around, opening her mouth to tell him that she, too, was about to phone everyone involved to tell them what had happened, when the sight of a bare wall stopped her.

Lucy had already noticed it a couple of times. It was the wall that greeted everyone at the end of the reception lobby as they entered the Calypso. At first, she'd thought it had needed an artwork of some sort, a painting maybe, something to draw the eye. Yet, in seeing it now, she knew exactly what would fit there—the perfect feature for that spot.

"Paul?"

Her sweet tone had suspicion contorting his features.

"Yes, Lucy?"

"I need your help with something."

Paul frowned, glanced at the bare, white wall and then back to her. His head tilted, confusion furrowing his brows. "What did you have in mind?"

Lucy grinned. It was a brilliant idea, the perfect gift of congratulations for the man she loved, the perfect way to honor him, their Calypso and Cal's wonderful father, Philip. All she had to do after securing Paul's agreement was make a few calls—the first of all to Toby.

There were so many stars. Lucy didn't think they would be able to see so many stars with all the lights of the hotel and the city of the Gold Coast around them. But there they were, glowing above her, twinkling down on the glistening, unsettled water of the swimming pool as she reclined in the large, plastic pool tire. Her head hung back loosely, staring up at the dark night sky as her arms and legs lay over the pink rim of the flotation device. Absent-mindedly, she traced circles in the cool liquid around her with her fingertips.

It was a little after nine, just under an hour before the Calypso's pool closed for the day. It had been another long day, but a very successful one. After getting confirmation from Paul about her project, Lucy had called Toby and asked him to email her as soon as possible with an important item. Although it had been quite some time since they'd last talked, around five years or so, they'd quickly slipped back into the easy, casual rhythm of good friends.

All those years ago, Toby had hated keeping secrets from Cal, hated what had become of his cousin's favorite friendship. For that reason, Lucy had done her best to distance herself from Toby as well, contacting him every now and then over the years, mainly via email or short text message, asking the usual—how he was doing and if he was well. She tried not to tell him too much, so that he didn't feel obliged to keep things secret from Cal, and then half a decade ago, Lucy decided it was time to let him go. She missed him dearly, but knew that his friendship with Cal, the enduring love he had for his cousin, was more important and she didn't want to do anything further to jeopardize it. However, this time, the secret she'd asked him to keep was one Toby had gladly agreed to. It had probably helped that all would be revealed in a matter of days and that the secret itself was one Cal was sure to adore, rather than something that might hurt him. Either way, she'd been appreciative of Toby's help and his compliance. Lucy may not have been able to tell Cal that she loved him just yet, even though she knew the feeling inside her was true, but this at least, the perfect thing she had planned, would do all that and more.

Suddenly, a cold, wet nose nuzzled into her neck giving her goosebumps and making her giggle.

"What's got you all deep in thought?" Cal spoke slowly, seductively making the words vibrate through her as his lips touched the skin of her throat.

Lucy giggled again and lifted her head, moving away from him. "Never you mind," she told him playfully.

In a quick motion, Cal spun the pool tire, with her in it, around in the water to face him. He offered her a charming smirk before raking his gaze down to her lips, her throat, her breasts, full and barely covered in her turquoise bikini. The coolness of his rough palms covered the warmth of her dry knees and then those sexy blue-grey eyes met hers again.

"Lucy, Lucy, Lucy," he purred as his fingers crept up her thighs. "I thought we were past keeping secrets."

"I don't know what you're talking about," she chuckled innocently.

Skeptically, Cal quirked an eyebrow and then moved closer to her, pressing his bare, wet chest against the pink plastic between her knees. Although at over six feet, he was taller than her in normal circumstances, in the water with her sitting in the tire, their eyes were almost level.

"If you don't tell me soon, Miss Spencer," he warned her softly. "I may have to interrogate you and, just so you know, you may not like my techniques."

Lucy bit back a smile as a little thrill of excitement jump-started her heart. "Oh, I think I might."

Cal's smirk became mischievous and his hands slipped down into the water around the top of her thighs before clasping the supple flesh of her backside. A feminine gasp of surprise escaped her lips at the delectable sensation of his fingers gripping her. Lucy giggled again, partly from nerves and partly in anticipation. Then, Cal was lifting her, pulling her toward him. As her knees slipped around his waist, her hands gripping the firm muscles of his shoulders, Lucy felt the tire pop out from beneath her and skitter across the water behind her. She was flush against his hard body now with only the top of her torso above the chilly liquid surrounding them. Her nipples pricked to attention as the water tickled her sensitive skin and the feel of Cal between her thighs had her insides aching.

"Are you going to tell me now?" Cal asked her, whispering the question, so close their lips were almost touching.

Lucy shook her head slightly, hoping her wide-eyed expression still held some innocence and hadn't been too clouded with desire. Wrapping her arms casually around Cal's neck, she pressed the soft line of her body closer to his, enjoying the warmth of his skin and the coolness of the water curling over her. When her breasts melted against the solid muscle of his chest, electricity radiated from their peaks, tugging at her tender nipples, and throbbing deep within her sensual core.

His smoky-blue gaze darkened as he stared into her eyes and then his lips were on her, nibbling at her jaw line and across to her ear. Lucy sighed at the deliciousness of it and let her head fall to the side to give him better access. Cal nipped at her earlobe before sucking it into his mouth and sending goosebumps across her skin. His lips moved to her ear, his soft tongue darting out to lick around the delicate flesh. Lucy gasped and tightened her grip around his neck.

"How about now?" Cal laid a kiss on her ear and then moved back down to her throat.

"Huh?" Lucy's eyes were closed as she relished the sensations vibrating through her, the tickles of electricity, the quivers of need, the ache of the hunger she had for him.

He chuckled, his mouth caressing her skin with the bounce of sound. "Distracted, are we? Come, come, Miss Spencer, we must stay on task."

Lucy lifted her head, causing Cal to do the same. She stared into his beautiful eyes and licked her lips. "I thought I was."

She didn't give him time to think over her answer, didn't give him time to think period. Lucy pressed her mouth to his and smothered him with the passion that was overwhelming her. She licked at his lips, his teeth and, when he opened to her, she let her tongue dance in the warm silk of his mouth.

Cal groaned against her, his grip on her derriere tightening before one hand snuck beneath the flimsy, wet material of her bikini briefs to caress bare flesh. Then he lowered her closer to the steel shaft of his erection and held her hard against him.

Lucy gasped into their kiss and then forced it to end. As she moved to lean away, Cal ducked forward, his mouth seeking hers again. She quickly eluded him and then touched her nose to his, caressed his cheek with hers, stroking her face lovingly against his just like an affectionate pet.

"We need to go upstairs," she told him, her voice barely a whisper.

His lips were against her ear again, sending shivers of desire down her body. "What's wrong with right here?"

For a second, she couldn't think of anything. Why couldn't they make love right here in the cool, wetness of the water? Then commonsense returned briefly.

"It's a public pool," she managed slowly.

Hearing her answer, Cal hesitated and Lucy thought—and hoped—he might be about to say that he just didn't care.

Then he nodded slightly, his face rubbing gently against hers. "Upstairs."

*

As soon as the door to his hotel room had closed, Cal had thrown their towels to the floor and started tugging at the end of Lucy's bikini, desperate to relieve her of it.

He had barely been able to contain himself the entire ride up in the elevator and Lucy knew she hadn't been much better. They hadn't even wasted time drying themselves off once they were out of the pool. It was obvious that neither of them could think much further than their main goal, the thing they had both craved since the first time they'd seen each other after so many years. She'd been fantasizing about it ever since they were teenagers, and she was certain Cal had probably been the same.

Lucy was grateful they had waited so long after re-connecting, even if it had initially been a hostile reunion. She was finally ready to accept him, to let Cal in, to open all of herself up to him. For better or for worse, she trusted him with her body and her heart and felt certain in her gut, in the feminine instincts that helped to guide her, that he was different, more mature, and that he loved her. Lucy wanted him, all of him, in her life, merged with her soul forever, and she was sure he felt the same.

Cal's coarse fingertips were kneading her naked breast, gently tweaking her sensitive nipple as he backed her farther into the room. She couldn't see where they were going, didn't care. His mouth was covering hers, consuming her. His kiss was passionate, overpowering, mind-blowing. Cal's other hand was working at undoing the thin bow ties of material at her hips, while her hands sought to remove his board-shorts.

The back of her knees hit the softness of a mattress as the turquoise fabric of her bikini bottom fell to the floor. Lucy legs gave way, instinctively collapsing her backward onto the bed and she lost her grip on Cal. She giggled as she bounced lightly on the cushioned top, her bare breasts bouncing joyously with the movement. When she looked back up at Cal, she noticed that she'd succeeded in undoing the tie on his shorts and opening the Velcro, but still they held their position low on his hips.

That just won't do, she thought to herself. She needed him naked and needed him naked—now.

With a smirk, Lucy propped herself on her elbows and gazed up at his face. Cal was staring down at her, his dark gaze raking over her body with such a carnal hunger that it forced a shot of adrenaline to race through her, pumping her heartbeat faster. She bit her lip and fought off the nervousness that tried to restrain her. Cal watched the movement intently, his gaze lingering on her mouth, before giving her a smug, catlike smile.

As if knowing he had her attention, Cal's hands moved to his hips, and he began to slip the board-shorts downward. Without too much effort, the pants slid down his legs, revealing the bold, solid length of his erection. Lucy's eyes widened, and she felt a pang of pleasure throb deep inside her, aching, anticipating him. It was enough to cause a warm, moistness to pool between her slender thighs.

Stepping free of the material, Cal bent his head toward her, placing a chaste kiss on her lips, then her jaw, and then her throat. As he moved to kneel before her, placing his warm hands on her thighs, Lucy felt herself groan in protest.

"I want you now," she all but growled at him.

Cal glanced back up at her and shook his head. "I've waited a long time for this, Lucy, and I plan on taking"—he bent and laid a kiss on her right nipple—"my sweet"—he kissed her left—"time."

As he bent lower, kissing a hot, wet line down her stomach, Lucy moaned and let her head fall back.

"Okay," she breathed.

Cal's jaw grazed her smooth thighs, the sandy five-o'clock shadow tickling her skin. Gently, he pushed her legs farther apart, revealing even more of the neatly trimmed little patch of dark hair that looked like an arrow head pointing the direction to her deepest pleasure.

With her eyes closed, Lucy held her breath, waiting, longing for that most intimate touch. And then Cal's lips were there, kissing, nibbling the soft, sensitive mound before delving deeper. His tongue slipped out to lick long strokes through heated flesh and Lucy moaned low in her throat. The sensation was ecstasy, tickling, building, her body throbbing. Cal's face dropped lower, farther between her thighs as the coarse stubble on his cheeks turned her smooth skin into shivering goosebumps.

Cal groaned hungrily as he tasted her, suckling her there, drawing a cry from her lips, before probing his tongue deeper, licking inside her, discovering all of her. The thrusts of his eager tongue moving rhythmically into her and out, mixed with the lazy kisses of his full lips on the silky skin outside was driving her crazy. Lucy couldn't hold out much longer. She ached for him, her whole-body yearning for him to fill her, for that final release.

"I need you," she whimpered. "Cal, I need you now."

Lucy couldn't move, she was lost to the passionate rhythm, to the deliciousness of his tongue searching inside her, melting her insides with each languid lick. She gasped and then the warmth of Cal between her legs disappeared. When she opened her eyes, he was above her. His lips returned to hers, tasting salty and sweet, like her, like him. Engrossed in the magnetism of their kiss, Lucy's hands roamed over his muscular chest and the fine, blond hairs scattered there, before linking around his neck.

All of a sudden, Cal's hands were around her backside and he was lifting her higher on the bed beneath him, continuing to kiss her as he did so. Once her head was resting on the cloud of fluffy white pillows at the headboard, Cal stopped and loomed above her. Reaching over to the nightstand, he opened the brown leather wallet laying there and retrieved a small foil packet. Ripping it open with his teeth, he freed the condom and threw the packet to the floor. After his hand had moved between them, slipping it over his thick, bulging arousal, Lucy pulled Cal's face back down to hers. Eagerly, her mouth mauled his, her kiss-swollen lips keen to caress his for eternity.

Cal groaned again and lowered the firm line of his body against hers. The head of his erection pushed between her thighs, seeking entry. Instinctively, Lucy spread her legs wide and then propped her hips up to reach him. She felt him stroke her and then slide slowly deep inside her, through the moistness of her velvet flesh. As Cal inhaled harshly, Lucy cried out at the heavenly sensation, the fullness, the feeling of Cal at home inside her. After pushing in to the hilt, he began a rhythmic motion, thrusting gently at first as deep as he could possibly go and then increasing the speed as their need grew.

Lucy's legs curled around him, pressing against his rump, pushing him in deeper with each pounding thrust.

Her hips rocked, dancing with his, interlocked with feverish desire. Cal kissed her, possessing her as the intensity built. She gasped, feeling bursts of electricity tingle through her, the growing rapture of climax nearing. Cal kissed her neck, her throat and Lucy cried out again, her chest arching, pressing her breasts, her sensitive nipples against his skin.

"Cal," she groaned, her breathing ragged.

His soft lips covered hers again, stealing her breath. She was suffocating, melting, losing control, becoming one with him. Her mind reeled, her body lost to the fiery heat, the wonder of their love-making. Her hands became claw-like, gripping the strong muscles of Cal's back as she hung onto him, desperately clinging to him so that she didn't float heavenward.

"Cal!" she cried out to him, as she felt herself slip, falling over the edge into the liquid warmth and the burning, blissful satisfaction of climax.

"I love you," Cal breathed and then tensed, his lips hovering over hers as he came.

CHAPTER FIFTEEN

A vibrating noise disturbed Cal from sleep, like the sound of plastic rattling against glass.

As he woke, he took a second to appreciate the sweet, fruity scent of Lucy's hair, before placing a gentle kiss against the soft, delicate strands. Raising his head, Cal glanced at the clock-radio on the nightstand. It wasn't yet two in the morning. When the disruptive noise continued, he looked around the room and then remembered that he'd left his phone on the glass-topped coffee table in the unit's lounge room after dinner, before they'd gone swimming.

Carefully, he lifted his left hand from where Lucy had had it cuddled between her bare breasts and then slipped out the right arm that had fallen asleep beneath her neck. She muttered something softly in her sleep when the warmth of his body left her. As Cal began to inch off the mattress, the vibrating noise stopped as quickly as it had started.

Irritated more by the fact that someone was ringing him at this ridiculously early hour than by having actually missed the phone call, Cal continued in his mission to find the phone. He wanted to see who'd had the nerve to disturb his sleep. Hopefully it had just been a telemarketer, someone who had a time-difference to blame their inconvenient timing on. But, Cal wanted to make certain.

Padding naked and barefoot across the carpeted floor from the bedroom to the lounge, Cal found his thoughts drifting back to events of the evening. Their love-making had been incredible, addictive, and earth-shattering. He hadn't been able to get enough. He'd barely let Lucy rest for five minutes after their phenomenal first time before ravishing her again. Cal had tasted her, all over, everywhere, but still couldn't sate his hunger for her. His body ached for her, wanting to touch her, needing to be inside her, to fill her with everything he had. He had made her scream out and cry in pleasure, and she had done her darnedest to make him lose his mind.

When she'd bent her head low and taken him into her mouth, her tongue swirling over him, her lips kissing, caressing, sucking, he'd thought he was going to die. The ecstasy had been so intense, had been beyond his wildest dreams of what it would've been like to have her make love to him in that way. It was irresistible, mind-blowing, and sucked the life right out of him until he could have sworn she was some kind of erotic succubus intent on stealing his soul. But, then he'd come, long and hard—and he'd wanted her all over again.

At the coffee table, Cal reached for his smartphone just as the screen lit up again and the device began to buzz against the glass top once more. Picking it up, he saw Jack's name flash across the screen. Puzzled as to why his good friend and his company's loyal financial advisor would be telephoning him at this hour, especially since they'd had an extensive but cheerful discussion only the morning before, Cal answered the call and put the phone to his ear.

"Jack?" Cal kept his voice quiet so as not to wake Lucy.

There was a deep, masculine sigh. "Cal—finally. You need to come home."

Fear gripped Cal's heart. Had something happened—to his mother, to Toby? "Why? What's wrong? Is my mother okay?" His voice was no longer a whisper.

Jack sighed again, this time sounding exasperated and exhausted. "No, Cal. It's nothing like that. Charmaine is fine. But we've got a problem. An emergency board meeting has been organized for later this morning."

On the other end of the line, Jack paused as though letting that news sink in before continuing. "Cal, a source is claiming that you've used company funds, not your own, to restore the Calypso."

An incensed guttural sound escaped Cal's lips, before he remembered that Lucy was sleeping only in the next room. "That is ridiculous," he growled, trying to keep his voice low.

Snatching one of the pool towels from where he'd discarded them on the floor earlier that night, Cal wrapped it around his hips and headed for the balcony door. Once he was safely outside in the crispness of the early morning air, overlooking the dimly lit pool below and the hushed roar of the Pacific Ocean beyond, Cal continued.

"Jack," he ground out his friend's name through gritted teeth. "You and I both know that I've only ever used my own private accounts to finance the Calypso's renovations. You're in charge of Hawthorne Incorporated's bankroll, for God's sake. You can prove to them that I haven't touched a cent. And why in heaven's name would I? I have enough money of my own to fund the marketing strategies and refurbishment of this complex and a hundred more like it before I'd even make a decent dent in my reserves."

"I know, Cal," Jack agreed enthusiastically. "You don't have to convince me. I've already prepared a statement for the board with proof that you haven't touched anything from the company accounts since you started this project."

"Then why I am being accused of such a slanderous fraud and summoned back to Melbourne in the middle of the night?" Cal's free hand had balled into a tight fist and he had started to pace angrily up and down the small, tiled balcony. His chest was tight, aching with confined fury, but he was doing his best to remain in control.

Jack exhaled loudly. "The information the source provided rattled a couple of our older board members, those fond of by-the-book behavior and hard evidence. As the source couldn't verify their claims, the board members are wary, but they need to hear it from you, Cal. They need to see the bills, the statements, proof of purchases, anything you have. Ultimately, their trust remains with you, most of them have known you for decades, but they feel obliged this time to ensure that your business methods remain above board."

Cal was infuriated at the idea, at the mere thought of the people on his board of directors believing that he was able to commit such a deception, but after a few deep breaths, he reevaluated what Jack had told him. Although it insulted him deeply to have anyone he'd worked with for so long—and who had worked alongside his father—believe him capable of something so horrendous, it did unfortunately make sense for them to be cautious. While he and his company had never suffered such an atrocious betrayal from an insider, many of them—including Cal, himself—had witnessed the downfall of other businesses from such a scam.

"Alright." The word left Cal's lips as a chilling growl. "I'll fly back tonight. I have some information here, but the rest I'll email you on the journey home. Print out everything and meet me in the boardroom at six to prepare."

"The board will be there at eight," Jack told him. "And I've already sent the company jet to the Gold Coast to fly you home."

Cal scoffed bitterly. "You sure the board won't have a problem with that too, Jack? Me using company assets and all?"

Jack laughed painfully. "Don't be a bastard, Cal. Your

board still trusts you and once all this crap has been sorted out, things will return to work as normal. They just need to be reassured."

Resignedly, Cal sighed. "It's a shame they couldn't just trust me outright."

Jack was stoically silent. "A transparent business is a successful one," he said softly. "The jet should already be at the airport. See you soon, Cal."

The line went silent as Jack ended the call and Cal lowered the mobile phone from his ear.

Glancing back at the closed glass sliding door that led into the unit's lounge room, Cal's thoughts turned to Lucy. What was he going to tell her? He couldn't just abandon her. Maybe she would sleep late and he could leave and return before she woke up? No, he had to tell her. But did he wake her? He didn't want to frighten her or have her worrying about him while he was gone, and he just didn't have time to explain everything. If she knew what was going on, she would want to come with him, he was sure of that. But, he wasn't quite ready for them to leave the Gold Coast, for them to leave the place that had finally brought them back together again. As soon as he'd finished with the board, he wanted to come back and when he did, he wanted to find her here, waiting for him—so that they could pick up exactly where they left off.

No, Cal had to go and Lucy had to stay behind. He would be back to her before noon if he could and he would have her naked and back in bed before she had time to kiss him hello. But he wouldn't wake her and he had to go now. He could send her a text message from the plane, explaining what he could without worrying her and that he'd be back on the Coast as soon as possible.

But, he had to go *now*.

***

"I love you."

Cal had said those three special words so many times during the night and it had filled Lucy with such delirious happiness that she'd almost said it back to him. Yet, she still hadn't found her nerve.

Cal held her heart, had her body, possessed her soul, but still a tiny part of her was fearful of his rejection, of his betrayal. She wanted to tell him, she really did. She was sure he already knew, yet she just couldn't. It hadn't been quite right, not yet. Although she knew they had moved beyond the past, that they were different people now, something inside her still needed him to understand, to know how deeply he'd hurt her back then. She wanted him to comprehend what he'd done and how dating all her friends, when he should have been dating her, had broken her heart. It seemed silly to expect something that in their current situation, their current relationship, seemed rather trivial, but it was what she needed. After that, Lucy was certain, there would be nothing holding her back from saying those three extraordinary words to Cal.

As Lucy's semi-consciousness mulled over the thought, pondering when exactly might be the right time, she began to wake up further. She reached across the bed for him, seeking the hot, solid body of the man it was so obvious she loved, but her fingers felt nothing except cool cotton. Reaching her arm out farther, she ran it deeper beneath the covers and then back up to slip beneath the fluffy cushioning of the pillows. Still, she found nothing. No warm skin, no silky hair, no heated indentation. As realization hit, Lucy opened her eyes.

Cal was gone.

***

The board meeting had been briefer than Cal had expected. It seemed that all the members were quite certain that Cal couldn't have been capable of what that secretive source was alleging. In fact, after quickly handing out the documented evidence that supported Cal's claims, the board of directors seemed more interested in hearing about his success with the Calypso rather than condemning him for it.

Many insisted that this be something they consider for other developments in their portfolio that had noticed significant decreases in profit largely due to the age of the property or lack of substantial marketing. After excited discussion, it seemed, everyone was hugely in favor of continued collaboration with Insight Marketing, with some board members even suggesting that Hawthorne Incorporated's own marketing team gather training and new ideas from the firm. Cal was more than overjoyed and when Jack called for a decision on the sale of the Calypso, the nays that answered were universal.

With a contented smile on his face, Cal exited his company's building just after nine. As he stepped out into the bright sunlight of the unusually cheerful Monday morning and admired the vigorous hustle of the busy Melbourne street, he noticed a familiar face.

Looking impeccable in his lemon-colored business shirt and black slacks, and with every dark hair on his head slicked back perfectly in place, Trent approached him. The insane, shark-like grin that split his face appeared aggressively smug, while the hands in his pockets and the casual stride of his walk implied a cool uncaringness that didn't quite match.

"I didn't realize you were in the habit of making house calls?" Cal couldn't stop himself from sounding sardonic.

Everything was starting to piece together in his mind, all the drama of the past evening, his board members' concerns, the unnamed source who had started it all. Cal was beginning to think he knew exactly who was responsible—and that the culprit was standing right in front of him.

"Did you think you could have it all?" Trent taunted as

he stopped in front of him. "Your company, the hotel?" He paused, his malevolent grin faltering slightly. "Lucy?"

Cal narrowed his gaze angrily. This self-obsessed prick was the reason he'd had to come back to town, the reason he'd had to leave Lucy behind—and because of what, his irrational infatuation with her? When was he going to get a clue and realize that he and Lucy, it just wasn't going to happen?

"So," Cal snarled. "I've got you to thank for my little detour this morning, do I?"

Trent laughed. "You don't deserve her."

"And you do?" Cal was fuming and had to dig his fingernails into his palms to keep from punching the asshole—or strangling him to death.

"I've never betrayed her," Trent spat confidently as his hands slipped from his pants pockets and became fists at his sides.

"Neither have I," Cal declared.

Trent's grin sharpened. "That's not what I've heard."

Cal felt his upper lip twitch, aching to form a snarl. What the hell did *that* mean? And what the hell had Trent *heard*? Cal had never betrayed Lucy, he loved her, he always had. He would never have done anything to hurt her.

He opened his mouth to roar back a snide retort when a mental cog in his brain clicked into place and everything, the last fourteen years, began to make perfect sense.

He *had* betrayed her. In fact, he had broken her heart.

The thought of it stabbed a painful ache right through his chest and into his own heart. No wonder she had spent fourteen years avoiding him. Back then, he'd been so focused on how much he'd loved her, how much he longed to be with her that he hadn't given much thought as to whether she truly loved him in return. As a teenager, he'd always believed that her love for him grew mostly from their friendship and so, the thought of altering that, of morphing it into something beyond pure and platonic, would eventually scare her away.

Cal hadn't wanted to hurt her, hadn't wanted to lose her and in turn, searched for a way to hide his own feelings. It was in that way, in dating all her girlfriends, that he'd ultimately betrayed her. Lucy had loved him, she'd always loved him and instead of giving their love a chance all those years ago, instead of asking a simple question— will you go out with me?—Cal had done the unthinkable and broken her innocent heart.

"What a jerk." The quiet words slipped from his mouth as he stared through Trent, his mind focused on his own revelation.

"What did you call me?" Fury contorted Trent's features and he stepped forward.

With a wave of his hand, Cal dismissed him. "Not you, you idiot. Me."

Puzzlement clouded Trent's vision and then he seemed to return to his previous focus. "Did you just call me an idiot?"

Exasperated, Cal raised his hands and glared at the insignificant man before him. "I don't have time for this."

As he moved to step around Trent, the slightly shorter man stopped him, moving in front of him to block his path again.

"We're not finished here," he growled at Cal.

"Keep your distance," Cal warned him, "or I'll be forced to signal for security to detain you."

His green eyes blazing with anger and obvious hatred, Trent scoffed in his face. "Afraid of me, are you? Afraid of getting your precious suit dirty?" He reached a hand up to Cal's collar and roughly straightened the black lapel of his suit jacket.

"Mr. Hawthorne, sir, do you need some assistance?"

Trent froze at the distant, yet intimidating sound of the authoritative voice.

Cal hadn't even bothered to signal security and yet, they'd been alert as ever.

"Mr. Hawthorne?"

Cal relished the familiar sound of Dave's voice, the security officer who usually manned the door to the Hawthorne building. He was friendly, astute and took his job very seriously. After this, Cal would have to look at giving the man a pay rise.

Raising an eyebrow as though in question, Cal stared at Trent, knowing full well that if he didn't answer Dave soon, he would leave his post at the front door to come and investigate.

Quickly, Trent released his lapel and stepped away. "We're not finished," he told him.

The sound of heavy footsteps nearing them made Trent's eyes widen and his behavior become skittish.

"Oh, I think we are," Cal told him, smugly. "Understand this, Trent, Lucy never loved you. She barely liked you. And if you ever come near her or me again, you can consider yourself sued for defamation."

Trent's jaw dropped and rage flickered in his eyes. "You can't do that."

Cal crossed his arms over his chest and then shrugged. "I'm pretty sure I have enough evidence to prove that it was you who accused me of using company finances to fund a private project," he bluffed.

Grimacing, Trent's green eyes grew large and then larger still when the looming, dark-haired security guard reached them.

"Is there a problem, sir?" Dave's hard gaze was trained on Trent as he moved to place himself protectively in front of Cal.

"N—no," Trent stuttered, his nervousness obviously getting the better of him. Then he looked past the menacing member of security staff, to glare again at Cal. "But I work with Lucy! I can't avoid her."

Cal grinned. "Get a new job, Trent."

Snide, entitled, conceited Trent suddenly looked helpless.

Never really as callous as he sometimes wished to

appear, Cal sighed. "If you're very lucky—and you behave," he advised Trent patronizingly, "I may just speak to Julia about organizing a letter of recommendation before you leave Insight Marketing."

Trent's gaze became distant as though he seemed to be weighing his options. His brows furrow fiercely and then he bit his lower lip, anxiously.

"Sir?" Dave began again, moving slightly closer to him.

As though anticipating the movement, Trent jumped back in fright at the same time.

"Okay, okay. I'm going," he told them both as irritation still contorted his angular features. He glanced one more time at Cal, his glare full of resentment. "I didn't really want her anyway," he lied. "She's damaged goods." With that he strode quickly away, leaving Cal and Dave watching his rapid retreat.

CHAPTER SIXTEEN

Sure, Lucy had seen Cal's text message—all three lines of it.

Cal: *Had to return to Melbourne for a last-minute meeting. Be back as soon as possible. Love you.*

Still, she didn't know what to think of it. When she'd first woken up alone, her heart had nearly broken all over again. She was certain that was it. Cal had gotten what he'd wanted, gotten to sleep with her, to collect the last notch in his bed-post from high school and then left. It had been what she'd been so afraid of, that he'd never really loved her at all and had always just been using her. She had felt like such an idiot. She'd wanted to scream, to cry, to smash everything in the room she could find. But instead, she'd done nothing.

She lay in the bed, his bed—just lay there. Everything had stopped, it felt like time had stopped, life had stopped. All she could do was breathe. Until eventually, a heavy feeling in the pit of her stomach had forced her to get up. It was dread, it was emptiness, it was a kind of absolution.

Cal had done it again. He'd betrayed her, ripped her heart right out of her chest and stomped on it while laughing, while telling her that he loved her, that they belonged together. It was the final treachery, the final injury. She'd given him everything, her mind, her heart, her body, her soul, and he'd made sure he'd taken all of them and left her with nothing.

She'd dressed herself, feeling nothing and then left his empty room for her own. That was when she'd seen the message. The tiny, three-lined text message that attempted to explain everything, but managed to explain nothing.

Had she been wrong? Did he actually care about her? Or was he just covering his ass? But then why wouldn't he have just left? Why send a text message with an explanation if he'd already gotten what he'd wanted? He could have easily just returned to Melbourne without a word.

Lucy was completely and utterly confused. Nearly every fiber of her being was telling her to trust him, that what they had together was exceptionally special, not something anyone would just throw away. Her heart argued that she knew he loved her, that he'd done everything he could to convince her. She'd felt it, he'd felt it, because it had been so exquisitely true. But her mind disputed it. Why leave her at all? Why not wake her and take her with him? Why not tell her in person, not via message? What was he hiding— the fact that he didn't want her, that he didn't really love her?

Her chest ached again and she rubbed her palm against it, over the delicate material of her summery, floral dress. Lucy was sitting in the reception lounge waiting for her taxicab to arrive. After much deliberation with herself, after the shame, the anger, the emptiness had overwhelmed her and then subsided, she'd finally decided that it was time for the holiday to end. It was time for her to go home.

Lucy had booked a flight back to Melbourne without telling Paul and then packed her things. When she'd exited the elevator and walked into the lobby just after one in the afternoon, she had been pleasantly relieved to discover that Paul was on his lunch break. Georgina, a twenty-something, mild-mannered brunette had gladly called the taxi company for her and requested a ride to the airport.

Glancing at her wristwatch, Lucy noted that it had already been fifteen minutes. The taxicab had either forgotten about her or would show up any instant. She looked back outside at the bright sunlight on the cement of the driveway leading to the street beyond. As she watched, a black limousine turned into the Calypso's grounds and parked beneath the shaded awning of the hotel's grand porte-cochere. The elegant car's back door opened and Cal stepped out, looking as handsome as ever in his black suit and white shirt.

Hurriedly, he ran up the couple of steps to the entrance and moved through the automatic glass door. As he walked further inside, his eyes met hers and his hard expression softened.

"Lucy." He'd said her name with such delighted relief that it tugged at her heart.

Still shocked by his abrupt appearance, by the fact that he'd really kept his word and that he'd actually returned to her, Lucy felt suddenly tearful.

"You left me." Her words came out with such agony that she just didn't have the strength to control her tears.

With her lower lip trembling, she blinked and droplets of water cascaded down her rosy cheeks. Cal's expression tightened with pain and he ran over to her. Reaching for her, he pulled her up from her seated position on the royal blue sofa and into his arms. He cradled her tightly against him until her arms wrapped around his back.

"I'm so sorry," he murmured, soothingly. "I love you. I'm so sorry."

Lucy gripped him tightly as her sobbing shook through her body, rocking her against him, while he continued to apologize and declare his love for her. After a couple of minutes, her emotions began to calm and her crying ceased, but still Cal held onto her.

"I'm sorry," he told her again, his tone gentle and affectionate.

Lucy nodded and finally managed to form words. "I know."

Hearing her answer, Cal pulled away from her just enough that he could see her face. He gazed down at her, remorse filling his blue-gray eyes.

"No, you don't," he said, his tone full of regret. "I'm sorry for everything, Luce. For leaving you here alone, for being such a jerk and for breaking your heart fourteen years ago."

Lucy's mouth opened at his acknowledgement and surprise widened her vibrant blue eyes. "What?" The sound that left her lips was just a whisper.

"I'm sorry, Lucy," Cal repeated. "I know I hurt you. I'm such a jerk, but I finally figured out what I did to push you away all those years ago. I've always loved you, Luce. I should've never dated all your girlfriends. It was a stupid idea. I can see that now. I was so terrified at the time, of losing you, of having you reject me if you knew the truth. I couldn't bear to lose our friendship and I'd thought that if I could hide it, hide my feelings in some way, then we could go on as normal and I would never ever lose you. I thought if you saw me with other girls, if you thought I was happy, content, you would never suspect that I loved you. I never wanted to ruin things, I never meant to break your heart, but in the end, I managed to do both."

Cal rubbed her shoulders lovingly and then held her tight against him again. "I'm so sorry, Luce. I love you and I'll never ever break your heart again."

With her face pressed into the warm, spicy scent of his neck, Lucy took a long moment to get her thoughts in order—and breathe him in.

He'd called himself a jerk, said he'd been stupid, but so had she. She'd actually believed he'd left her, that he'd abandoned her after they'd slept together, because that was all he'd wanted from her. It was such a ridiculous thought now that it nearly made Lucy laugh.

If she'd been paying attention when he'd first stepped back into her life, she would have seen that the Cal she'd once known, once hated so very much that she'd loved him all the more, had actually matured. He was no longer the kind, considerate child who would do everything and anything to keep everyone else happy, no longer the young boy who wanted to please, who was terrified of real conflict and who always tried to keep the peace. No, this man before her had grown. He was no longer scared, he knew what he wanted, and he was willing to fight for it. He no longer sought attention or felt the need to be liked by everyone. He was comfortable with himself, with who he was, strengths, weaknesses and all. He was stable, honest, and ready to apologize and take responsibility for his mistakes. And above all, he was capable of loving as deeply and as wholly as everyone else—even her.

Smiling into the delicious skin of his neck, Lucy breathed him in once more and then kissed him there.

A sound vibrated through Cal's throat, almost a purr and then he pulled away from her again, so that he could gaze down at her. "Do you forgive me?" He asked the question with such desperate need, such fragile confidence that Lucy's heart ached for him.

Lifting her face until their lips met, Lucy placed a quick, gentle kiss on his mouth. She stared up into his eyes, losing herself in their beauty, in their depths, in his soul. "I love you," she told him.

Bliss brightened the blue-grey orbs of his gaze and his breath caught in his throat. "You do?"

Lucy touched her nose to his affectionately and then slipped her arms around his neck. "I've always loved you," she told him and then she giggled lightly. "I never admitted it to myself back then, and you never admitted it to me. I guess that makes us both jerks."

Cal laughed. "Seems like we were made for each other then."

Lucy licked her lips. "You know what that means," she asked him, cautiously.

His brows furrowed.

Lucy grinned. "You're stuck with me." Then she shrugged nonchalantly. "Forever."

With another burst of laughter, Cal covered Lucy's lips with his own. His kiss engulfed her senses, overwhelmed her, completed her, until Lucy gave into the heavenly sensations and melted against him—their two bodies becoming one.

***

It was finally Friday the first of May. The Calypso had been officially saved from sale, with the necessary documents having all been approved and signed off on by both Cal and the rest of Hawthorne Incorporated's board of directors. Insight Marketing had been retained for a number of new contracts with Cal's company to repeat their successful methods in improving and promoting a few more unappreciated, less profitable hotels. Julia had also informed the Insight Marketing staff, and Cal for good measure, that Trent was leaving the team and had decided to join another advertising firm in Sydney.

Yet, the good news hadn't stopped there. It had been three days since Lucy had declared her love for him and then finally agreed to the fact that they were now formally dating, and to celebrate, Cal had invited Steph and Mia to join them for a special Dreamworld weekend. Lucy had told him how eager her friends had been to visit the theme park and he'd seen it as an opportunity to make the surprise he'd had in store for her all the more special.

But, now Lucy was being secretive again. This time she'd actually blindfolded him. She wouldn't tell him anything more than that he had to cover his eyes with the narrow piece of black material before she would take him downstairs. In the elevator on the way to the ground floor, he'd heard Mia and Lucy giggle between hushed whispers, but hadn't been able to distinguish any clear words. As they'd stepped out into the lobby, Lucy's soft, feminine hand was holding his again.

"This seems way more kinky than necessary." Cal heard Steph chuckle to the right of him.

Lucy shushed her as she continued to lead Cal forward. "Be grateful I didn't blindfold you too. After all, you haven't seen it either."

As Steph made a snorting noise, Mia sung, "But, I think I know what it is."

"So, it's an *it*," Cal said ponderingly.

Lucy squeezed his hand affectionately in hers and he felt the warmth of her body move closer to him. "We're nearly there," she told him. "So, you'll just have to wait and see."

Cal smiled to himself. At least whatever *it* was, it was something worth getting excited over.

"Okay." Cal heard Lucy say as she stopped him. "Here is good."

There was a surprised gasp from Mia, but Steph quickly hushed her with a few whispered words.

As Lucy gently pushed at his muscular side, Cal followed the silent instruction and turned slightly to the left. After taking a deep breath and removing her hand from his, she undid the blindfold.

When the smooth fabric fell away from his eyes, Cal had to blink a few times to adjust his vision to the bright, fluorescent lights of the reception lounge. Then, he saw it.

"Whoa," he breathed.

It was almost life-size, nearly six-foot and covered the majority of the once empty, white wall at the end of the reception lobby, the wall that greeted every guest as they entered. The high-contrast image of various shades of black and grey that filled the massive sheet of thick glass was very familiar, one of his father's favorites, and was made all the more impressive with the glow of the white paint behind. Bolted solidly to the wall, the original photograph of Phillip Hawthorne and Cal as a young boy walking along Main Beach with fishing rods in hand, had been enlarged and delicately etched onto the huge piece of pristine glass. They were both looking at each other, smiling, laughing. It had been a wonderful day, Cal could still remember it well. He could even make out the tail of one of the fish they'd caught in the bucket in the sand in front of them. Toby had taken the photo. He'd stayed put to look after the gear, while Cal and his dad had gone to try another fishing spot a little farther down the beach. They had been good times and Cal had been especially lucky to have had a father like Phillip.

As he stared, dumbstruck by the awesome image in front of him, the magnificent gift, Lucy wrapped an arm around his waist and cuddled close to him.

"Do you like it?" Although there was still a great deal of excitement left in her tone, there was also a tiny lilt of uncertainty.

"A...are—" Cal choked on his words as his throat tightened.

He'd known he'd felt overwhelmed, known his heart had swelled at the sight of the fond memory, but he hadn't realized that he'd become emotional. He blinked back the blurriness that suddenly filled his vision and quickly wiped at his eyes.

For God's sake, he was a grown man. There was no need to cry over a photograph no matter how tender the meaning behind the gift was and no need to bring up old emotions at the remembrance of his father. He could appreciate the touching nature of Lucy's present and the glorious memories it ignited without crying about it.

With a steadying breath, Cal tried again. "Are you serious, Lucy?" He turned toward her and took her into his arms. "It's incredible! I can't believe you did this for me." He cleared his throat as emotion threatened to overpower him again. His hand shot back up to his eyes to wipe away anymore telltale dampness, before his gaze settled back on Lucy's face.

"It wasn't just me," she replied as tears began to well in her eyes, even though her smile remained wide, elated and content. "Toby and Paul helped."

"I love it," Cal grinned, "and I love you." His fingertip brushed away a droplet as it freed itself from her eyelashes and started a moist trail down her cheek. "Don't cry, darling," he told her sweetly, his loving smile mirroring hers.

She rolled her eyes at him attempting playfulness. "Easier said than done."

He chuckled and then placed a soft kiss on her luscious lips.

"Get a room." The teasing tone of Steph's voice interrupted their serenity.

Lucy broke their kiss with a laugh. "We're getting comments from the peanut gallery."

Humorously, Cal sighed. "Who invited them anyway?" He glanced back to where Steph and Mia were standing, huddled close together, a little way behind them and then winked. "That's right, I did."

"At least you've learned for next time," Lucy joked, bringing his attention back to her.

"Actually," he said carefully as he began to back out of their embrace, "I invited them for a reason."

Still smiling, Lucy's gaze narrowed. "Oh?"

"You're not the only one," Cal purred, "who had them keep a secret."

Suspiciously, Lucy looked between the three of them and then her stunning, tranquil blue stare settled back on Cal.

"Since I wasn't about to leave your side a second time," he told her wisely, "I had to ask them to make a detour on their way here from the airport, to pick up a special order I'd pre-arranged." Glancing over at Steph, he held out a hand to her.

With an innocent look at Lucy, she shrugged, waited a minute and then, with a grin, she retrieved a little blue jewelry box from the back pocket of her jeans. She stepped forward to hand it to him and then—Cal dropped to one knee.

Lucy's hands shot to her cheeks, to cover her mouth and her eyes grew large and round with shock. "No— what?" Her words were gasps.

"Lucy Spencer," Cal said formally, as he opened the ring box and held it out to her, "will you marry me?"

Her jaw dropped. She covered her face with her hands and then looked at Steph and Mia before glancing back down at Cal. "Are *you* serious?" The question she posed was similar to his earlier remark.

Cal chuckled and then nodded. "I've never wanted something, never needed something, never loved someone as much as I love you, want you and need you in my life. Luce—my Lucy—I've always loved you and always will. Marry me and make my life complete."

Lucy gasped again, then nodded excitedly as new tears filled her beautiful blue eyes. "Yes!"

Cal sprang up off the floor and lunged at her, wrapping his arms around her, enveloping her in the tightest of hugs as he kissed her forehead, her cheeks, her lips. With that one word, she had made all his dreams come true. His heart swelled so much that he felt as though pure joy might just burst from his chest. His veins burned with rapture, with adrenalin, with absolute pleasure.

"I love you," she told him between kisses. "I love you."

They broke apart just enough for Cal to remove the exquisite, white diamond ring from its box and slip it on Lucy's finger. With Cal's help, Lucy wiped away her hot tears and stared down at the precious gem set in gold. As her right hand covered her mouth once again in shock, she held her left hand up a little and glanced over at Mia.

Cal watched on as they seemed to share a look of hidden understanding and then Mia, with a mischievous grin, held out her own left hand. A similar ring with a rose-gold band and a different cut diamond was wrapped around her own fourth finger.

Lucy took a sharp breath of surprise and her eyes brightened with glee. "Oh my God," she cried and then stepped forward to embrace her friends.

After hugging each of them tightly, Lucy turned back to Cal. "Did you know about this?" Her voice was still full of shock and excitement.

He nodded, joyfully. "When I'd called Steph, once they'd arrived at the airport, to ask if she would help me with my own proposal, I found out that she'd proposed on the plane ride here."

"It was time," Steph explained, when Lucy looked over at her. "I had always wanted it to be different, to be special." Her smile beamed. "Mia just loves flying and has always wanted to go to Dreamworld, so I thought what could be better?"

Mia cuddled up to Steph and kissed her cheek before returning her attention to Cal and Lucy. "We were thinking New Zealand, maybe next spring and you're both invited, of course."

Chuckling, Steph grabbed Mia's hand. "Come on, babe, let's give these two a moment alone." As Steph began leading her fiancé toward the elevators at the end of the lobby, Mia turned back to look at them.

"You've got ten minutes," she teased them, "and then I want to be sitting in a taxicab and heading to Dreamworld."

Steph sighed in playful exasperation and then pushed Mia into an open elevator after a young family hurried out.

Lucy and Cal laughed as the lift doors closed and then they turned their attention back to each other. Cal slipped his hands around her waist, toying with the band of her jean shorts just below her pink blouse, while Lucy's arms wrapped around his neck.

"So, you love me, do you?" he asked her with his tone

a little impish.

She shrugged and gave him innocent eyes, fluttering her long dark lashes at him. "Maybe?"

Smirking, Cal pulled her closer, his hard body in his khaki shorts and black t-shirt flush against hers. "So, you want to marry me?"

Lucy grinned, but her gaze remained sweet and virtuous. "Seems like it."

Cal felt pure delight fill him, his chest swelled and his heart felt strong and powerful. Lucy was finally his as he had always been hers. Fate had pulled them together again and now he would never let her go.

"You see, Mr. Hawthorne," Lucy told him, a seductive tone lowering her voice an octave, "it seems you've already forgotten." She moved her mouth closer to his, so that her lips tickled him as she breathed. "But, as I told you the other day, you're now stuck with me—forever."

Cal chuckled, his lips brushing hers. "What a hardship," he lied. "How will I ever bear it?" Then his mouth covered hers in a blissful kiss and they were lost to the intense sensations, to the lustful passions, to the ultimate true love that was and always would be their destiny to share.

The End

IF YOU ENJOYED THIS BOOK, CHECK OUT TAMMY'S OTHER BOOKS...

Invited by one brother, tempted by the other...

Former Australian playboy Blake Davenport knows his billionaire brother, David, is capable of anything to ensure he gets what he wants. But manipulating his young daughter's beautiful teacher into marriage is unacceptable.

Gwen Deveraux is grateful for the invitation to spend Christmas and New Year's with her beloved student's family, especially when her handsome host is so eager for her company. After surviving a broken heart, she is finally ready to give love another chance.

But, who with?

The illustrious David Davenport whose real motives

seem hidden behind charm? Or his roguish brother, Blake, who has tempted her heart and body from the very moment they met?

Seven romantic tales of love where royalty, celebrities, and passion meet. A case of mistaken identity, protecting the one you love, or proving you aren't all about the money...these tales will entice and thrill.

A Royal Pain by Abigail Drake

Getting shot in the bottom saving a visiting royal turns out to be the best thing to happen to, impoverished socialite, Chloe Burkhart in a long time, especially when the prince's very handsome, very sexy bodyguard, Nicolai, comes to her aid.

Caught by Him by Tammy Mannersly
Blockbuster movie actor, Brody Nash doesn't quite know what to make of the gorgeous woman precariously perched on his neighbor's gate, but as they start to get to know each other better, he begins to wonder if she might just be the *one* for him.

Romancing the Princess by Bridie Hall
A commoner, Sebastian, and Princess Alixandra are set to get married until he begins to wonder if fitting in with royalty is worth sacrificing his principles. Love rules all. Or does it?

All My Memories by Grea Warner
The possibility of reconnecting with an unrequited love leads country music star Finn Murphy on a journey of memories in this special prequel to the Country Roads series.

Me and Tillie by Lisa Hahn
1950s musical film star Oren Cooper returns to Broadway to find new inspiration. Unexpectedly, that inspiration comes in the form of Tillie Parker—his childhood friend's little sister and an up-and-coming ingénue.

Defending Demma by Melissa Kay Clarke
When faced with an unsavory past, can Demma St. John, rising new starlet, trust ex-Marine Ryker "Digger" McMillan with her secrets and her heart?

His Royal Typeface by Stephanie Keyes
When all is lost, love can be found. Will Prince Asher Tarrington's unique font design be enough to salvage a royal family and set the tone for true love?

ABOUT THE AUTHOR

Tammy Mannersly is an Australian author based in Brisbane, Queensland. She loves writing romance, has a fondness for animals, is crazy about movies and enjoys a great Happily Ever After. Her passion for writing started from a very young age and lead her to complete a Bachelor Degree in Creative Industries majoring in Creative Writing at Queensland University of Technology. You can find out more information about Tammy and her work on her website: www.tammymannersly.com or by visiting Facebook: https://www.facebook.com/profile.php?id=100013727268166 and Goodreads: https://www.goodreads.com/user/show/60685325-tammy-mannersly.